The
CLEOPATRA LOOK
...WAS GONE,

along with the metal breastplates that had formed the top half of her costume. Without them she looked sweet, vulnerable—and very naked.

"*I'm a girl given to sudden decisions,*" *she said throatily.* "*And I've decided to do you a favor, Danny, with no strings attached. Just to show there's no hard feelings because you wouldn't give me the tape.*"

"*You've been spying on my dreams,*" *I said.*

"*Turn around,*" *she whispered.* "*A girl looks like a fool taking off her pants when there's a man watching.*"

I turned, and suddenly found myself on my knees. There was a nasty swishing sound near my head, and then a yelp from Liz as she hit my shoulder with her knee. . . .

SIGNET Thrillers by Carter Brown
(50¢ each except where noted)

THE NEW AMERICAN LIBRARY, INC., P.O. Box 2310, Grand Central Station, New York, New York 10017

Please send me the SIGNET BOOKS I have checked above. I am enclosing $_____(check or money order—no currency or C.O.D.'s). Please include the list price plus 10¢ a copy to cover mailing costs. (New York City residents add 6% Sales Tax. Other New York State residents add 3% plus any local sales or use taxes.)

Name_____

Address_____

City_____ State_____ Zip Code_____

Allow at least 3 weeks for delivery

MURDER
IS THE MESSAGE

by Carter Brown

A SIGNET BOOK

Published by
THE NEW AMERICAN LIBRARY
in association with Horwitz Publications

SIGNET TRADEMARK REG. U.S. PAT. OFF. AND FOREIGN COUNTRIES
REGISTERED TRADEMARK—MARCA REGISTRADA
HECHO EN CHICAGO, U.S.A.

*SIGNET BOOKS are published by
The New American Library, Inc.,
1301 Avenue of the Americas, New York, New York 10019*

FIRST PRINTING, DECEMBER, 1969

PRINTED IN THE UNITED STATES OF AMERICA

MURDER
IS THE MESSAGE

Chapter
ONE

The living room was vast, with open French doors leading out onto a spacious terrace. A harvest moon hung suspended in the clear night sky, serenely oblivious to its competition from the sparkling crystal chandeliers inside the penthouse. I took time out in the doorway to light a cigarette and orient myself. It looked like either most of the guests were running late, or the party was going to be a strictly intimate affair. A group of three men were huddled in one corner, deep in conversation, while a lone brunette silently communed with her martini in the center of the room. She turned around as I came close and the visual impact hit me right between the eyes.

Her long brown hair swirled freely around her naked shoulders, making a perfect frame for her oval-shaped face. The dark eyes held a kind of smoldering sensuality that fit real well with the savage twist to her wide mouth. Her flawless skin was tanned a deep copper color and—except for the metal breastplates—she was naked from the waist up. White satin culottes fit tight over the surge of her hips and hugged her rounded thighs, then finally flared into a bell-bottomed fantasy around her ankles. Without even closing my eyes, I could see the both of us floating leisurely down the Nile, with never an asp in mind.

"Hi!" I gave her my left profile which is just a fraction

better than my right, and therefore perfection. "I'm Danny Boyd."

"I'm Alysia Ames," she said in a deep throaty voice.

"I had you figured as Cleopatra," I told her. "Like, who else would buy her bra from the local hardware store?"

A wanton gleam showed up in her dark eyes as her fingers briefly caressed the metal cups. "I'm just crazy about the way they hold me," she confided in a husky whisper. "Tight! Like a pair of hands—male hands, of course!—I have a strictly heterosexual imagination."

"Me, too," I gulped, "and this has to be the first time I've ever visualized myself as a stand-in for a couple of tin plates."

"I guess we're both in love with our own profiles," she chuckled. "The only real difference is that mine is situated a little lower down." Her face stiffened suddenly as she stared over my left shoulder. "So man the lifeboats, Captain," she said obtusely. "I can see a torpedo heading right this way!"

I saw the blonde bearing down on us and had to admit the look on her face was somehow reminiscent of a warhead, rapidly ticking its way through a five-second fuse. Her bourbon-colored hair was stacked high on top of her head in a kind of elaborate cone, and a feathery fringe stopped short an inch above her stormy blue eyes. The narrow top lip and over-full bottom lip were compressed tight into a petulant pout. She was wearing an ankle-length white lace-knit dress with a button-up front, and a mandarin collar. It looked the height of modesty until she got real close, then the lace knit was revealed as a collection of holes loosely strung together so they gave a total see-through effect. Underneath, she was wearing a white lace bra over deep full breasts, matching briefs, and the rest was delicious pink-and-white flesh.

"Well!" She bared her teeth at the brunette. "I didn't

8

know Stirling had planned a whore's picnic for tonight until I saw you were here, Alysia."

"Why else would he invite you, Shari?" the brunette purred. "But you must meet Mr. Boyd. The both of you should get along famously together; from the way he's been talking, he's almost as sex-starved as you look, darling."

The blonde gave me a quick grimace which was maybe meant to be a smile, then said, "I'm Shari Wayland."

"Wife—in name only—of our absent host," Alysia Ames added maliciously.

"Just where the hell is Stirling, anyway?" Shari Wayland demanded in a tight voice.

"The new butler said he'd been unavoidably detained, but he'll show up later," the brunette said idly. "I didn't know he was back from the Coast already. He was supposed to be spending the whole week there."

"I wouldn't worry, even if he has brought a new mistress back with him," the blonde said in a saccharin voice. "He's sure to pension you off with a generous settlement!"

"Do you think you're wise to wear a see-through dress, darling?" Alysia Ames asked in a sympathetic purr. "I mean, it does reveal that ghastly problem you have with all that—intimate?—acne!"

Their glances locked, and I figured any moment now the whole thing would degenerate into a nail-scratching, eye-gouging brawl. I smiled neutrally at the both of them, then beat a swift retreat to the bar. Three quick gulps of a seven-to-one martini soothed my strung nerve-ends, and I relaxed enough to light a cigarette. A little time later, a tall cadaverous-looking character fronted up at the bar beside me.

"My name's Stanger," he said in a reedy baritone. "Kurt Stanger."

"Danny Boyd," I told him.

9

"I wonder what the hell Wayland thinks he's doing." He poured a meticulous measure of Scotch into a glass, added one ice cube, and about a spoonful of soda water. "A matter of life and death, the invitation said, and then he doesn't even show up on time!"

"I wouldn't know what he's at," I said truthfully. "I've never met Mr. Wayland before."

His faded speckle-brown eyes stared at me suspiciously from beneath shaggy black eyebrows. "You must be joking, Mr. Boyd?"

"Like you said, the invitation said it was a matter of life and death." I shrugged. "I found it kind of irresistible."

"Wayland never does anything without some good reason," he said sourly. "I wouldn't give the conniving son of a bitch the time of day, without consulting my attorney first."

"He's not a friend of yours, exactly?" I prodded.

"Only a business associate." His tone of voice made it sound like some kind of an unspeakable disease. "Thrust upon me against my own wishes and better judgment. Wayland has built himself a spurious reputaton as a troubleshooter in the corporation world. I happen to be the president of *Strategic Developments Corporation,* and we have a problem right now. Wayland has been called in to resolve it, over my head." He took a quick bird-like sip of his Scotch. "Undermined from within by the executive vice-president of the corporation, Mr. Boyd! My dear friend, George Thatcher, made goddamned sure he had the numbers before we entered the boardroom." He nodded toward the two men talking animatedly in the far corner. "Judas George is the one on the left."

Thatcher looked someplace in his late thirties; tall, with an athletic build, and a full head of wiry black hair. His rugged face had a deep tan, and I could see the flash

10

of his white teeth even across the length of the room. The way he was dressed, it looked like he'd just dropped in for a quick martini before stepping back onto the front page of *Esquire*.

"Who's the guy with him?" I asked.

"Ed Norman, Wayland's junior partner." Stanger pursed his thin lips into a thinner line. "A nasty little man."

"He looks like he's six feet tall," I said.

"Oh, very well!" He sighed gently. "A nasty big man."

The impeccable-looking Jeeves buttled his way across the room toward us. "Excuse me, gentlemen," he said in an impossibly-British voice," but a package has just been delivered for Mr. Boyd. If you would follow me to the study, sir?"

"I do hope something macabre has happened to Wayland," Stanger said with a kind of morbid relish in his voice. "If the package contains both his index fingers, or such, promise me I'll be the first to know, Mr. Boyd."

"Sure," I agreed. "And if it starts ticking, I'll even let you open it first."

I followed the butler out into the huge front hall, and then into one of the side rooms. The small neatly-wrapped package sat on top of a leathercovered desk. There was a gentle click as the butler closed the door in back of me. I walked across to the desk, unwrapped the package, and came up with three separate items; a letter, a check made out to me for a thousand dollars, and a pocketsized tape recorder.

The letter read:

Dear Mr. Boyd,
The enclosed check is a retainer for your services. When the other five guests are present, I wish you to play them the tape on the recorder. You will find the message

11

is self-explanatory and also contains my further instructions,

> *Sincerely,*
> *Stirling Wayland.*

So I had some kind of a nut for a client. I put the letter and the check carefully into the inside pocket of my coat, and figured the thousand dollars retainer entitled him to believe he was Bugs Bunny for all I cared. Then I picked up the tape recorder and took it back into the living room. Stanger looked mildly interested when I placed it on the bartop alongside my unfinished drink.

"No index fingers, Mr. Boyd?" He sounded disappointed.

"Wayland has sent us a message," I said. "He wants me to play it for the assembled guests."

He took another quick bird-like sip of his Scotch. "How fascinating! If I can't have chopped index fingers, I suppose I'll have to settle for a deranged mind." He turned around from the bar, clapped his hands together sharply, and the chatter died a sudden death. "Gather round, everybody," he commanded. "Wayland has sent us greetings by way of a tape recorder!"

The two women came across the room quickly, their eyes shining with curiosity, while the two men took their time about joining the group clustered around the bar. Stanger made the introductions, and Judas George Thatcher flashed his brilliant white teeth at me in a kind of automatic reflex. Close up, Ed Norman was tall and skinny with thinning blond hair, and light blue eyes set close on either side of a thin pointed nose. His face was set in a tight mask, and I idly wondered what was bugging him so much it was making him lose weight and his hair?

"It must be Stirling's idea of a joke, or something?"

Shari Wayland said in an incredulous voice. "Sending a tape recording to his own party!"

"I guess this will be the second practical joke he's made in his life," Alysia Ames purred. "The first was when he married you, darling."

"Why don't we listen to it and find out?" Norman asked abruptly.

"Why not?" I pressed the button and the reels started to revolve slowly. Stanger took another quick sip of his Scotch, then bent his head toward the machine attentively, and I waited to see his ears twitch.

"Good evening," said a deep bland voice. *"This is Stirling Wayland speaking, and I regret I cannot be with you in person tonight. My invitations said it concerned a matter of life and death. As everyone, with the lone exception of Mr. Boyd, knows, I have been on the West Coast. The night before last someone tried to kill me."*

"What a goddamned shame they missed!" Shari Wayland said softly.

"He must be drunk, or crazy?" Thatcher grunted.

"Shut up and listen!" Stanger told him angrily.

"If you have all now finished with your various ejaculations?" the recorded voice sneered. *"The details are unimportant at the moment but I shall recount them later to Mr. Boyd who, incidentally, is a private detective I've hired to ensure I stay alive."* A sudden cold ferocity gave a sharp edge to the formerly bland voice. *"I am convinced that one, or more of the five people with you right now, Mr. Boyd, was behind the murder attempt."*

"He's flipped!" Alysia Ames whispered.

"Did somebody suggest I must be out of my mind?" The voice chuckled softly and I saw the brunette's face whiten under the deep tan. *"Let's talk about motives, Mr. Boyd,"* the voice continued, *"and I suppose it would only be polite to start with the ladies first? The only bond left between me and my estranged wife is one of mutual*

13

hatred. She desperately wants a divorce, and it gives me exquisite pleasure to deny her wish. I have a certain hold over her which makes it impossible for her to divorce me. Perhaps she's gotten tired of waiting around for me to drop dead from natural causes?

"Then there's my mistress, Alysia Ames, who's become so bored with me she's been playing house with my partner, Ed Norman. With me out of the way, they wouldn't have to be furtive anymore, and young faithful Ed could take over the business. Don't let that nervous look of his fool you, Mr. Boyd. Underneath, my junior partner has a will of steel!.

"Finally," the voice harshened again, *"we come to the two most incompetent men who ever ran down a healthy corporation into the garbage disposal unit. Stanger knows right now that the only way out is by a merger, and this is what I'll recommend. When it happens, he'll be out so fast his feet won't touch. It was through Thatcher's connivance that I was called in as the consultant, and you could mistakenly think him a friend of mine. Actually, he's a friend of Ed Norman, although they've gone to a hell of a lot of trouble to hide the fact. Old college buddies, and both with the same ambition to replace their respective bosses!"*

The machine hummed silently for a couple of seconds while the five of them watched it intently, like they were all willing it to burst into a sheet of flame.

"As I told you before, Mr. Boyd," the voice resumed, *"I shall be in touch with you soon. I'm engaged in some secret research at the moment, and the end result could prove to be very interesting indeed. Meanwhile, I want you to keep this tape recording in a safe place for future reference."* A sardonic note of amusement crept into the voice. *"Before I sign off, I'd like to thank everyone for coming tonight. I'm sorry I can't be with you, because*

14

from here on out I imagine it's going to develop into a real fun-type party!"

A moment later the tape ran out. The click, as I pressed the stop button, made an explosive sound in the deep silence that immersed the room. Stanger took a quick peck at his Scotch, and it made me wonder if just the one drink lasted him a whole week. Thatcher and Norman just stood there with expressionless faces, like they were only waiting for the next bus. Shari Wayland turned toward the brunette with a tigerish smile on her face.

"I wonder that you don't catch cold, darling," she said in a deeply sympathetic voice. "Leaping from one warm bed to the other, the whole time!"

"I'm fascinated by this certain hold Stirling has over you," Alysia Ames replied sweetly. "I never thought anyone else would ever guess—except me—that you're a female impersonator."

"Ladies!" Stanger held up his hand like a traffic cop. "Please, let us not digress from the important problem that concerns us all. Wayland—let us be charitable!—has presumably suffered some kind of a brain seizure." His bony index finger pointed toward the tape recorder on the bar. "Should that libelous and defamatory rubbish fall into the wrong hands, it could do us all untold harm." His eyebrows met in a shaggy line. "I think it should be destroyed, right here and now."

"You're right, Kurt," George Thatcher said crisply. "Imagine what would happen if any other member of our board heard it!"

"I agree," Norman said, blinking his eyes rapidly. "Those wild accusations could completely undermine our professional reputations."

"Especially Alysia's, darling!" Shari Wayland chuckled throatily.

I replaced the top on the mini-recorder, then put it into

15

my coat pocket. "My client said for me to keep it in a safe place," I told them, "and that's what I figure on doing."

"Sorry, Boyd." Thatcher flashed his white teeth at me. "We can't afford to let you do that."

"How will you stop me?" I asked politely.

"By force, if necessary," he grunted.

"You want to give it the good old college try it's okay by me," I told him. "I'm leaving now."

By the time I had taken a couple of steps away from the bar, Thatcher was standing directly in front of me with a fixed grin on his face. I kept heading straight toward him and he swung a punch at me with his right fist. It was slow and clumsy, giving me all the time in the world to step outside it and make a grab for his wrist. My fingers grabbed air as he pivoted gracefully on one foot and, the next moment, the edge of his other hand slammed brutally across the side of my neck. The impact knocked me sideways, then the edge of his right hand across the other side of my neck straightened me up again. I had about a split second to wonder if my neck was about to snap off clean at the shoulders, then his stiffened fingers sank deep into my solar plexus and I started to fold like a jack-knife.

"So I fight dirty," Thatcher chuckled, "but it's winning that counts. Right, Boyd?"

I was too busy fighting to get some air back into my lungs right then to bother trying to answer him. The edge of his hand slammed down across the nape of my neck, driving me to my knees, and I made a frantic grab for the floor as it started to lurch away from me.

"*Hold it!*" An authoritative voice said from what sounded a long way away.

The floor slowly tilted back to the horizontal after I had shaken my head a couple of times. I kept the flat of my hands pressed against it in case it tried to sneak off someplace again, then very cautiously lifted my head. It was only the impeccable-looking Jeeves standing in the doorway who had spoken, I realized. Then I vaguely wondered what the hell a butler was doing with a gun in his right hand?

"The party is over," he said in a conversational voice, "and everyone except Mr. Boyd is leaving right now. And don't try to be a hero, Mr. Thatcher, or I'll put a bullet through one of your legs!"

Chapter
TWO

"They've gone." He moved around the back of the bar and set up two glasses. "How are you feeling now, Boyd?"

"Mortified, mostly," I admitted. "Thanks for helping out. I'm supposed to be a professional and all, and he took me like I was some little old lady on one of her off days!"

"It can happen to anyone," he said easily, then pushed a glass across the bartop toward me. "Try some of Stirling's thirty-year-old Scotch. It's guaranteed to be therapeutic!"

"Thanks." I swallowed some of the mellow liquor, then looked at him. "It came to me like a sudden flash of genius—the moment I saw you holding that gun—buttling is only a sometime thing with you, right? And whatever happened to that phony British accent?"

He grinned. "Did it sound that bad? I kind of thought it went with the butler's outfit. I'm an old friend of Stirling's who owed him a favor—Chuck MacKenzie. He

17

called me from the Coast three days back, explained what he wanted and that he was airmailing the tape, and would I set up the party for him."

"You sent out the invitations?"

"And needed to be around to make sure all the guests were here, before I gave you the tape and your instructions." The grin faded from his face. "I'm worried about Stirling. He was supposed to call me last night, and didn't. I called his hotel—the Ambassador—late this afternoon, and they said he hadn't checked out, but they hadn't seen him since yesterday morning."

"Maybe he's busy with that secret investigation he mentioned?" I suggested.

"Maybe. I don't pretend to know what this is all about, Danny, but I do know Stirling Wayland. He's not given to being fanciful, or playing wild games just for the hell of it. If he says somebody is trying to murder him, I believe it." MacKenzie knuckled the tip of his nose gently. "I'm not supposed to tell you this, but I'm holding a certified check for five thousand dollars from him, to be given you in the event of his death in return for a full-scale investigation by you of the circumstances."

"Where is he on the Coast, exactly?" I asked.

"A small resort town called Santo Bahia. I guess you know it?"

"I know it," I said, and winced. "There's a certain Lieutenant Schell of the local gendarmes who loves me like a brother. And I do mean the brother who stole his life savings, then ran off with his wife!"

"Stirling said you had quite a reputation down there," he grinned, "that's why he wanted you for the job."

"You figure I should go look for him in Santo Bahia, Chuck?"

"I guess it's theoretically none of my business, but I figure you should," he said carefully. "That's where the trouble is, too."

"Trouble?"

"Where *Strategic Developments* has acquired its big problem. Stanger and Thatcher have been in town the last couple of days trying to borrow their way out of it, but nobody will touch them with an asbestos glove! So they'll be heading back to Santo Bahia tomorrow, most likely, and so will Ed Norman."

"What kind of a problem do they have, exactly?"

"Up until now they were always land developers," MacKenzie said. "But this time they came up with a grandiose kind of scheme to not only develop the land, but do the building themselves, too. They bought fifty acres that had a river frontage, cleared and landscaped it, then encircled it with a canal so they turned the land into an island. The intention was to build a country club right in the center, then surround it with real exclusive homes that would sell in the eighty-thousand-dollars-plus bracket. They figured for snob appeal it would have just about everything; the purchaser would be living on his own island, with his own country club near by, and there was swimming and boating waiting for him at the bottom of his own backyard."

"So what went wrong?" I queried.

"Just about everything! They hit rock where they didn't expect to hit it—the county demanded three bridges instead of the one they'd previously agreed to— there was an unprecedented rainfall that put back their schedule a couple of months. I could go on and on, Danny, but it all adds up to the point that they just ran out of money before they could complete anything that was salable at a profit. The corporation is mortgaged up to its neck already, and its creditors are about to start filing suit."

"If, like Wayland said on that tape, a merger is the only out for them," I said, "why is Stanger so against it?"

"Because he'll be out on his ear, as Stirling also said,

19

for one thing. Even more important to him is he's a twenty percent stockholder in the corporation, and he suspects that any merger Stirling organizes would leave him with a vast capital loss."

"Okay," I said. "So I'll fly out there tomorrow and see if I can find Wayland."

"Where will you stay?"

"The Ambassador hotel, where else?" I told him. "Where can I contact you?"

"I'll contact you," he said decisively. "Maybe I'm already sticking my nose into something that shouldn't concern me, from Stirling's viewpoint."

"Are you in the same line of business as Wayland?" I asked idly.

A sardonic gleam of amusement showed up in his polished blue eyes for a brief moment, then he shook his head. "Nothing like that! And, incidentally, don't forget to stash that tape away someplace safe."

"Sure." I finished my drink and slid off the barstool. "Well, thanks again, Chuck."

"My pleasure," he grinned. "You mind letting yourself out, Danny? I guess I'd better stick around and clean up the apartment a little."

The harvest moon was still riding high in the sky when I got out onto the street, and the humid night air closed around me like a wet blanket. I picked up a cab before I had walked one block, and it was only five after ten when I was back inside my own pad on Central Park West. A long hot shower eased the stiffness in my neck, and gave me time to think about the whole crazy evening. It was no trouble to recall the faces of the five guests in clear detail, but whenever I tried to visualize Chuck Mac-Kenzie's face I drew a complete blank. The best I could come up with was a kind of Wodehouse stereotype, and I knew he hadn't looked like that at all. I was out of the shower and just about dry when the door buzzer sounded off.

I went into the bedroom, put on a robe, collected the Thirty-eight from the top drawer of the bureau and slipped it into the pocket. So the pocket sagged a little with the weight of the gun. What the hell? I figured I preferred to be sartorially dead, than the real thing. Then I went to the front door and, feeling real brave, opened it a couple of inches. Maybe she had left her barge in the elevator, because there was just Cleopatra standing there with a hesitant smile on her face. I opened the door a little wider, like about eighteen inches, and told her to come on in. She stepped into the front hall and waited until I had closed the door again.

"I got you out of bed?" she queried.

"Just the shower," I told her.

"I wouldn't have disturbed you, but it's urgent." She took off the white satin cloak and handed it to me. "I won't keep you long, Mr. Boyd."

"Danny," I said.

"Danny." Her dark eyes smoldered a little. "Alysia is a stupid name. Most of my friends call me, Liz."

"Let me make you a drink, Liz?" I said.

"I'd like that." She gave me a long appraising look. "Is all that hair on your chest for real, Danny?"

"It has to go back in the morning," I said. "I get a reduced rate for nightly rentals from a little old wigmaker, who grows mushrooms in the basement."

We went into the living room and I made a couple of drinks, gave her one, then took mine into the bedroom while I slipped out of something loose and into a raffia shirt and a pair of slacks. I checked the profile in the mirror. It looked its usual superb self, so I gave it a friendly smile and a cheery wave of my hand before I went back to the living room.

Liz Ames was sitting on the couch with her drink in

21

one hand, and a cigarette in the other. A moment later she crossed her legs, and the white satin culottes made a soft whispering sound for a moment there. I wistfully wondered if those metal breastplates would make a ringing sound if she ever did the hula.

"I want a favor from you, Danny," she said. "I want to hear that tape over again?"

"All of it?"

She nodded fiercely. "All of it."

It wasn't my idea of a love-in, exactly, but the longer she was in the apartment, the more time she had to properly appreciate the profile. I brought the mini-recorder out of the bedroom, set it up on a coffee-table, and pressed the button. She listened intently, her eyes hidden under drooping lids, until the bland voice bade its farewell for the second time. I switched off the machine, sat down in an armchair facing her, and drank some of my rye while I waited.

"Thank you, Danny," she said finally. "Have you ever met Stirling Wayland?"

"Not yet," I told her.

"I don't think that is his voice," she said simply. "It's a very clever imitation, I'll admit, but it's still a fake."

"Why would anybody bother?"

"I don't know." Her wide mouth set in that savage twist again. "But I've been thinking damned hard ever since I heard it the first time in Stirling's apartment. That bit about me making time with Ed Norman isn't just a lie, it's a goddamned insult! I'd sooner go to bed with the first available doorman, than with that overgrown rabbit." Her eyes held mine with a commanding look. "Being any man's mistress is strictly a sometime thing, Danny. If Stirling lost interest in me tomorrow, I'd be left with the money he banked for me at the beginning of the month, the apartment lease paid up to the end of the quarter, a

22

few pieces of jewelry—an expensive wardrobe—and that's all! The situation would be exactly the same if he died tomorrow, so why the hell would I ever want to kill him?"

"It depends on who's telling the truth about Ed Norman—you?—or the voice on the tape?" I said.

"I can make a smart guess about who's been playing house with Floppy-ears Norman," she snapped, "and it's that Shari bitch!"

"The voice said something about Wayland having a hold over her, so she couldn't divorce him?" I queried.

"I wouldn't know what it was," Liz said, "but I guess it's true. From the moment I became Stirling's mistress, he's taken a great delight in flaunting me in Shari's face. She could have gotten enough proof about us for a dozen divorces by now."

"It still leaves us with the original question," I said. "Why would anyone bother faking Wayland's voice to make that tape?"

She drank slowly, then gave me a brooding look over the rim of her glass. "I guess this will sound real wild, Danny, but suppose Stirling is already dead? Suppose somebody killed him, then faked his voice on that tape, and set up the so-called party for tonight? He would know the body would have to be found sooner or later, and you'd turn over the tape to the police. That would be giving them five instant suspects, right?"

I grinned at her. "Like you said, Liz, it's a real wild idea."

"Don't worry about wild ideas," she said coolly, "I have loads! How come Stirling suddenly decided to employ you, and your butler friend, for example? I always figured private detectives were supposed to be tough guys, but after the way Thatcher beat the hell out of you with no trouble at all?" Her derisive gurgle of laughter rasped

23

my nerve-ends painfully. "You came on more like some fashion-designing fag, than a private detective!"

"So I underestimated Thatcher," I grated. "It won't happen a second time! And what makes you think the butler was a friend of mine?"

"The way he pulled a gun on Thatcher—Jeeves to the rescue—and, incidentally, made goddamned sure nobody had a chance to destroy the tape."

"You have a nasty suspicious mind, Liz." I took the letter, that had been part of the package deal waiting for me in Wayland's study, out of my wallet and gave it to her. "I guess you should know his signature?"

She read the note quickly and handed it back to me. "It looks genuine. But then, anybody who could fake Stirling's voice so cleverly, could probably do the same with his signature."

"I don't see how there's room for you to be clasping an asp to your bosom," I sighed. "But it's there, for sure!"

"There's one easy way you can prove you're on the level, Danny," she said casually. "Either give me the tape, or let me watch while you destroy it?"

"Fun is fun," I growled, "but, like one Siamese twin said to the other, what you're asking is impossible."

She shrugged her bare brown shoulders. "I don't see how I'm asking too much, Danny? The tape is a phony, anyway." The pink tip of her tongue slowly moistened her wide upper lip, while her dark smoldering eyes slowly burst into flame. "I'm a very practical girl, who'll gladly repay the favor in a very practical kind of way."

"I'm tempted," I said in an understatement, "only the man paid me a thousand dollars to keep his tape someplace safe, and not let people like you get their cotton-picking hands on it."

"So I guess I can't win them all." Liz got up onto her feet. "Can I use the bathroom?"

"Sure," I said. "It's off the bedroom, and that's the door right in back of you."

Her hand reached down to pick up her jeweled evening purse from the couch and—for a split-second there—time seemed to freeze. I watched her fingers clamp around one end of the purse and waited for her to lift it, but for that split-second just nothing happened. Then she used both hands to pick up the purse and held it clutched tight to her bare midriff. The unexplained pause had to be some kind of an optical illusion, I figured, and maybe I should have a doctor check out my liver real soon?

"I won't be long, Danny." She gave me a gracious smile, then headed toward the bedroom.

I filled in the hiatus by freshening up the drinks, then settled back into the armchair. Maybe a couple of minutes later, I heard her voice call my name in a soft caressing lilt. I turned my head in time to see her start walking toward me from the bedroom doorway, and the demure look on her face was the biggest lie of all time. She still had the purse clutched tight to her midriff, but there was one vital difference to the way she had looked before; the metal breastplates were missing.

"Sometimes they get to hold me a little too tight," she murmured, "so then I like to bounce free for a while."

Her conical-shaped breasts jutted forward at almost a rightangle to her torso, their milky whiteness making a startling contrast to the copper-colored tan surrounding them. They jiggled softly with each step she took, and I saw the small nipples were firmly-pointed. She stopped a couple of steps away from me, and I suddenly found I was standing up.

"I am a girl given to sudden decisions," she said throatily, "and I've decided to do you a favor, Danny, with no strings attached. Just to show there's no hard feelings about the tape?"

"You've been spying on my dreams," I told her.

"Turn around for a moment," she whispered. "I always think a girl looks a goddamned fool taking off her pants, when there's a man watching."

I turned around and, a split-second later, the explanation for that other split-second when time froze exploded inside my head. My reflexes were quicker than my conscious mind, and I suddenly found myself down on my knees. There was a nasty swishing sound above my head, followed by a kind of gargling yelp from Liz as her knee hit my shoulder and she pitched forward face-down onto the seat of the armchair. The purse flew out of her hand and landed with a heavy crunching sound on the floor. When I picked it up and felt its weight, I felt goddamned glad it hadn't connected with the side of my head the way Liz had intended. Inside, tucked carefully into one corner of the purse, was a formidable wedge of silver dollars.

The brunette stayed right where she was, her face buried in the cushions of the armchair, and her rump protruding high in the air. She suddenly burst into a flood of noisy tears and I figured if anybody was entitled to burst out crying it was me, with relief.

"Ah, shut up!" I told her, and slammed my open palm down hard across her white satin rump.

She let out a highpitched wail of pained surprise, then the tears became even noisier than before. I sat down on the couch and filled in the time while I waited for her to quiet down by finishing first my own drink, then hers. After what seemed a hell of a long time, the sobbing subsided into a series of sniffles, until she finally straightened back up onto her feet and shuffled slowly around toward me. She looked the way the heroine of the *Thousand And One Nights* must have looked on the thousand and second morning. Her eyes were red, her cheeks blotched and tearstained, and her lips ragged where she had chewed off most all of her lipstick. There was nothing sexy about her semi-nakedness anymore,

26

only a look of pathetic vulnerability. I tossed the white satin coat to her and she put it on quickly, then folded her arms tight across her breasts like she figured if she had to keep company with a mad-dog rapist, this was the best approach.

"That slap hurt!" she said accusingly.

"If you'd connected with that weighted purse, you could have killed me," I said reasonably.

"If you'd only given me the tape in the first place, it wouldn't have happened and we could be making love now," she snarled.

Logic to a dame must have about the same value as a bra does to a man, I figured; they both know the thing exists, but what the hell use is it to them?

"My God!" she moaned. "I must look like something even the cat wouldn't drag in. Give me back my purse, so I can go and get cleaned up a little."

I reluctantly handed her the purse, after I had removed the wedge of cartwheel dollars. "Don't be too long in the bathrom, Liz," I told her. "Because when you get back you're going to tell me exactly why you want that tape so bad."

"All right," she said in a tired voice. "Anything you goddamned well say, Danny!"

It took five minutes before she reappeared from the bedroom. Her hair was neatly brushed, her face had a scrubbed look, and the fresh lipstick had been evenly applied. Her white satin coat was open down the front, and I could see the metal breastplates were back in place.

"Maybe this letter will tell you what it's all about," she said in a calm voice.

"Letter?" I queried.

"In here."

She put her hand inside the jeweled purse and it came out holding a gun. It was a Thirty-eight Magnum and I could have quoted the serial number, even—what the

27

hell?—it was my own gun she was holding! The same gun I had left in the pocket of the robe tossed onto the bed, I remembered bitterly. It looked like it was time I quit the private eye business and got into some other line of work, something I could handle like shoveling snow off the sidewalk.

Liz Ames backed off until she reached the coffee-table, the gun barrel still pointing directly at my chest. She put her purse down on the table, found she couldn't manage both it and the mini-recorder with her free hand, so settled for the recorder.

"Take off your clothes," she said briskly.

"You've got to be out of your mind!" I growled.

"You heard me!" she snapped. "I'll use the gun if you don't do as you're told, Danny."

The look in her eyes said she wasn't kidding, and the thought of what a .38 slug could do to my manly chest quickly overcame my outraged vanity. I stripped down to a pair of jockey shorts, then looked at her pleadingly.

"Those, too," she grated.

She had said something about a girl looking like a goddamned fool, taking off her pants while there was a man watching her. The reverse situation not only made a man look and feel a goddamned fool but—my mind whimpered and quit thinking right there as I stepped out of my shorts and dropped them onto the floor.

"Well?" Her eyes looked me up and down with a meticulous attention to detail. "The physique isn't bad." She gave a husky ribald laugh that seared what was left of my personal vanity like a branding iron. "But I'm a little disappointed in you, Danny. I just don't inspire you at all, do I?" She gurgled with laughter again. "I can tell, just by looking!"

Then she turned around and ran quickly out of the room, and I heard the front door slam a couple of seconds later. The phone rang just after I'd gotten back into my clothes, and was still mouthing mild obscenities.

"Chuck MacKenzie, Danny," a cheerful voice said. "I've heard from Stirling Wayland, so I figured I'd better call you right away."

"He's okay?" I asked.

"Apparently he's had some success with his secret research, whatever that was. I told him what happened at the party tonight, and he still wants you to meet him at the hotel in Santo Bahia tomorrow."

"Fine," I grunted.

"He also asked me to check that you had that tape stashed away someplace real safe?"

"I've left it with a—" I almost choked on the word "—friend, somebody I can trust completely."

"That's good." He hesitated for a moment. "Don't get me wrong about this, I mean, I know you're a professional and all! But I meant to warn you earlier about that Ames girl. She's not only smart, but vicious, too!"

"Thanks, Chuck," I muttered from between clenched teeth, "I'll try and remember that."

"I guess it's stupid of me to even mention it," he chuckled. "You can probably handle her with both hands tied behind your back."

I hung up, and remembered Liz Ames not only had the tape, but also my gun, which was a kind of ultimate insult. Then I remembered she'd been forced to leave her purse, which was some kind of an exchange, at least. I upended the contents of the purse onto the coffee-table, and found a couple of interesting items. Her driver's license, which gave her address in the low East Fifties, and a bunch of keys on a jazzy platinum keyring. For sure the key to her apartment was one of those on the keyring, so she would have had to get the building superintendent to open up the apartment for her when she got home. Then, I figured, she would remember where she had left her

29

purse, and the first thing she'd do once she got inside the apartment would be to put the night-chain on the door. But it was still worth a try because I had nothing to lose but sleep.

The cab dropped me outside the apartment building some twenty minutes later. It was a five story walk-up in a block between First and Second Avenues, and it somehow didn't fit with that Cleopatra image at all. Her apartment was on the top floor, and when I arrived outside the front door I had a queasy feeling in the pit of my stomach; my imagination running riot and picturing her waiting just the other side of the door with my Thirty-eight in her hand. I could see the headlines already—*Private eye turned burglar gets head blown off in first caper!*—and my mind started whimpering again.

After a couple of unsuccessful tries, the third key fit the lock. I turned it, gave the front door a gentle push and it swung wide open. The moment after I stepped inside the apartment, I closed the door again even more gently and leaned my back against it. A bright rectangle of light spilled into the living room from an open doorway, and I crossed my fingers that she was in the shower, or someplace equally convenient. I catfooted across the front hall into the living room, put my back against the wall at one side of the open doorway, then took a quick peek inside the lighted room.

Liz Ames was sprawled out on the bed fast asleep, her face buried in the cushion, and still wearing her Cleopatra outfit. Halfway across the room my foot kicked against some hard object, and I felt a hell of a lot better when I saw it was my own gun. I picked it up and put it into my hip pocket, then went over to the bed. She didn't respond to my hand shaking her shoulder vigorously, so I finally pulled her over onto her back.

Her wide open eyes stared sightlessly at me, and blood still oozed sluggishly from the bullet hole high in her left

temple. For a long moment I just stood there s...
down at her body, then my mind started functio...
again. I yanked the Thirty-eight out of my hip pocket an...
confirmed that sinking feeling a couple of seconds later.
There was an empty chamber under the hammer, and
only five slugs left. It needed no genius to figure out the
sixth slug was buried inside the Ames girl's head, and I
was holding the murder weapon in my hand.

I checked out the apartment as thoroughly as I could
in ten minutes, and didn't find either the mini-recorder, or
the tape. So it was almost sure her murderer had taken
them with him. It left me with a hell of a lot of questions,
and no answers. The murderer could have been her ac-
complice and that's why she hadn't worried about leaving
her purse in my apartment, because she knew the accom-
plice would be waiting inside her own apartment and
would let her in? Or maybe he'd had another key, and
had arrived when she was out? Or—what the hell difference did it make?—it still left me right behind the eight
ball! The only thing I could do now was get the hell out
of there fast.

Suddenly, Santo Bahia sounded like a great place to
visit, and I couldn't wait to board the plane first thing in
the morning. But why stop there? Why not keep right on
going to someplace like Rio, or Buenos Aires? There was
only one way to resolve the problem, I realized, and that
was to find Liz Ames' murderer, before New York's finest
got to me first!

Chapter
THREE

"Room seven-two-eight," the desk clerk said brightly. "You'll like it, Mr. Boyd. It has a wonderful view of the whole waterfront." He turned to the pigeon hole briskly. "There are a couple of messages here for you." He beamed as he put them on the desktop in front of me. "Nice to have you back with us again. Santo Bahia's been a dull little town since the last time you were here."

The first message said Mr. Wayland would call me around six P.M., and the second said for me to call a Miss Milne in room seven-one-seven immediately after my arrival. Who she? I wondered, then my mind caught up with that last crack from the desk clerk.

"How can any California resort town be dull?" I asked him. "When you've got all this wonderful sunshine twenty-four hours a day?"

"Believe me, it can be very dull, Mr. Boyd." He leaned across the desk and lowered his voice to a confidential whisper. "But now you're back, I'm sure things will start to liven up again. Leastwise, Lieutenant Schell seems to feel the same about it."

"Schell?" I stared at him. "What's he got to do with it?"

"Did I say Schell?" His eyes were widely innocent.

"It's blackmail," I grunted, "and for ten bucks I want to know about both Schell and Miss Milne."

"You just used a nasty word, Mr. Boyd," he said in a reproachful voice, "and if you want double the information then you have to pay double the price."

"Who said piracy was dead?" I took two ten dollar bills out of my wallet, and the desk clerk neatly lifted them out of my fingers the next moment.

"The lieutenant visited around lunchtime," he said. "He wanted to know the moment you checked in, and asked me to keep an eye on your comings and goings, and the people you're seeing during your stay."

"He's a stockholder, he rates all these special services?" I snarled.

"He's a cop," the desk clerk said simply. "There'll come the time when we need a favor from him."

"How about this Milne dame?"

"A blonde," he said dreamily. "Beautifully stacked, with a pair of legs like—" he shook his head "—just wait until you see them, Mr. Boyd! She checked in a couple of hours back, from L.A."

"I could find all that out by checking the hotel register, then taking a look at her," I grated.

"There was one other thing. She asked if you'd made a reservation right off, then asked if she could have a room straight across the hall from you, as a special favor."

"You must be making your first million all in the one day!"

He smiled. "I'll agree it has been one of my better days, Mr. Boyd. If anything else comes up I think could interest you, I'll be in touch. The name is Sam Brickhouse."

"Okay, Sam," I said. "You do that."

He tossed the roomkey to the hovering bellhop. "Mr. Boyd is in seven-two-eight, Pete." Then he smiled warmly at me. "It's people like you who put the fun into the hotel game, Mr. Boyd!"

Five minutes later I was alone in the room, admiring the view of the coast line, and trying not to wonder if Liz Ames' body had been found yet in New York. My watch said it was ten after four, and the three hours time difference would make it early evening in Manhattan. I had about a couple of hours to wait for the call from Wayland, so I picked up the phone and asked the hotel operator for Miss Milne in room seven-one-seven.

"Jackie Milne," a warm contralto voice said after the second ring.

"Danny Boyd," I told her.

"I'm so glad you're here, Mr. Boyd. Did you have a nice trip?"

"I don't know," I said, "whenever I fly, I keep my eyes shut tight the whole time."

She laughed easily. "You obviously need a drink. Why don't you come on over and have one? My room's straight across the hall from yours."

"It cost me ten bucks to find out you'd organized it that way," I said. "How much did it cost you for the organization?"

"The same," she answered promptly, "and I should have known right off that little desk clerk was a fink!"

"I'll have a seven-to-one martini," I said.

"Coming up."

I knocked on the door of her room a short time later and the rich contralto voice told me to come on in. The blonde waiting in the living room of the suite with a welcoming smile on her face was everything the desk clerk had said, and more! Her strawberry-blonde hair had been cropped short so it fit sleekly to the contours of her head. Brilliant sapphire-colored eyes were set above high cheekbones, and the bold curves of her mouth were a living monument to sensuality. She was wearing a blue silk shirt that clung to the deep breasts that were set wide part on her torso, and an itty-bitty skirt that had been pasted onto her hips. The hemline covered maybe four inches of her thighs, and left the rest of her beautiful brown legs on view for the appreciation of a confirmed lecher like me.

"I knew there had to be some good reason for me

34

coming to the West Coast," I said, "and now I'm looking at it."

"It's been a long time since I've met a man who could make me feel I was wearing a see-through dress and no underwear," she said thoughtfully. "It does my ego good. Why don't we start off on a first name basis, Danny? I'm hoping we can be friends, even if we do have opposing interests." She gestured toward the nearest chair. "Won't you sit down?"

I sat down and she delivered the martini, then sat opposite me and cradled her own drink in her hands. The mini-hem had hiked up a little as she crossed her legs, exposing a further couple of inches of rounded thighs.

"Opposing interests, Jackie?" I queried.

"You're working for Stirling Wayland," she said evenly, "which means you're working for a bastard. I'm working for his wife, which means I'm working for a bitch." She shrugged gently. "Shari called me first thing this morning and told me what happened last night. She was sure you would be coming to Santo Bahia, and the chances were you'd stay at the same hotel where Wayland was staying."

"You're in the private eye business?" I asked incredulously.

She shook her head. "I guess you could call it industrial espionage, but it's not nearly so melodramatic as that sounds. It's a small select outfit that operates with people, instead of bugging devices and all that junk. If you want to find out what your competitor is being so secretive about, you come to us. We make a careful study of the personnel directly involved with whatever's secret in your competitor's organization, and then we get to one of them. It's always that simple, although the getting to one of them part can sometimes be quite complicated."

"You mean you blackmail somebody in the rival organization?"

"Highly unlikely!" She gurgled with laughter. "Most probably we offer them a better job with our own client. The trick is to pick the right man first off; pick the wrong one and he blows the whole thing to his president, and the organization is alerted to what you're trying to do."

"How does all that tie-in with Shari Wayland?"

"It doesn't," she said flatly. "I thought you should know a little of my background, Danny, is all. Shari's an old friend, and she's also become a client since this morning. She's worried about what exactly her husband is trying to do. So she asked me to come here and find out."

"How do you figure on doing that?" I asked.

"Don't forget that industrial spying is my line of work," she said confidently. "Once I can get a perspective on the true situation between *Strategic Developments* and Wayland, it shouldn't be too hard to figure out Wayland's angle."

"Suppose he's genuinely concerned that someone is trying to murder him?" I said. "And that's the only reason he made that tape?"

"Then I'll tell Shari that, and gracefully fade out of the picture." She smiled at me warmly. "I wouldn't try and compete with someone like you, Danny, in your line of work. That's the only reason you're here? To protect Wayland from someone who's trying to murder him?"

"What else?" I said.

"I hoped you'd tell me." She sipped some of her martini. "If there isn't any other reason, I can't see why we shouldn't work together on this? While I'm digging into the corporation background, there's a reasonable chance I could come up with the reason why someone wants Wayland dead. I just might come up with the name of the person involved."

"Sure, why not?" I agreed, then lifted my glass. "Here's to the partnership of Boyd and Milne."

"Milne and Boyd!" she grinned, then lifted her glass in

response. "Now that's fixed, what do you propose to do?"

"Right now, nothing but wait until Wayland calls me sometime around six tonight," I said.

"I have a date tonight with somebody who can give me a lot of the background to the whole development scheme, and what's gone wrong with it. Why don't we get together later on tonight and compare notes?"

"Sounds like a great idea," I acknowledged. "How about eleven o'clock?"

"And here in my room," she said. "Now, if you'll excuse me, Danny? I have to go bathe the body beautiful and put on a new face for my date."

"Sure." I stood up, finished my drink and put the empty glass back on top of the bureau. "Just one thing before I go, Jackie? You know what kind of a hold Wayland has on his wife, that she can't divorce him?"

She got up onto her feet, her hands absently smoothing the mini-skirt down over swelling curves of her hips. "Hold over Shari?" Her sapphire eyes were suddenly interested. "She's never told me anything about that."

"That's what he said on the tape," I told her. "I figure it must be true, because he flaunts his mistress in front of her the whole time, apparently."

"Alysia Ames," she nodded.

"You know her?"

"Only of her, from Shari's occasionally letting off steam about her. She was just divorced when Wayland found her." Her lips curved into a smile. "Her husband got back from out of town unexpectedly one weekend and found a kind of Roman orgy in progress; just five people involved—four husky young men—and Alysia!"

"It must have been one hell of a shock for the husband?" I grinned back at her.

"I guess it was. The way Shari tells it, he went straight into his study, collected his gun and his camera, then made them carry on with the orgy while he took a whole batch of flashlight pictures. Then he tossed the young men out of the house, and was generous enough to allow Alysia to put on some clothes first before he threw her out, too. He didn't even give her a dime for carfare!"

"Just tossed her out into the cold, cold snow?" I said.

"It never snows in Santo Bahia," she said. "Not that Charles MacKenzie would have given a damn if there'd been a blizzard raging outside."

"Charles MacKenzie?" I repeated.

"You know him?"

I shook my head. "I guess I've heard the name before someplace?"

"He runs a construction outfit, just about the biggest around here. I've never met him, either; I got the whole story from Shari who gets an enormous satisfaction out of repeating it—including all the more salacious details!—whenever she gets the chance." Her smile slowly faded. "You'll have to go now, Danny, or I'll never make my date on time."

"See you around eleven tonight," I said. "Have fun."

"This date is strictly a working assignment," she said in a soft voice. "I prefer to take my fun in private after the working day is finished." Her eyes had a bland innocent look in them as she stared hard at me. "In our line of work we both need to be very discreet about how, and with whom, we take our fun. Don't you agree, Danny?"

"Sure," I nodded, "and the next time I come into your room I'll walk backward, so if anybody sees me they'll think I'm coming out."

I went back to my own room and ordered a bottle of rye and some ice from room service. After it had arrived and I had made myself a drink, I checked out the number of the *MacKenzie Construction* outfit in the phone book and called it. When the switchboard girl answered, I told her my name was Milne, I wanted to speak with Mr. Charles MacKenzie, and my business was personal.

38

Around five seconds later a harsh masculine voice barked, "MacKenzie," into my ear.

"My name's Milne," I said. "I'm a private detective involved in an investigation that concerns your ex-wife, and I'm hoping you can give me a lead as to where I might find her?"

"We were divorced just over a year back," the voice snarled. "From the moment I threw that cheating broad out of my house, I haven't given a goddamn if she's alive or dead! My only advice to you, Mr. Milne, is that you'll most likely find her flat on her back wherever she is. It's her favorite hobby!" Then he hung up forcefully.

The voice didn't sound like the voice of the amateur butler in Wayland's penthouse the previous night. So maybe there were two Chuck MacKenzies, or the amateur butler had preferred to use that name instead of his real name? Like everything else that had happened so far, it didn't seem to get me anyplace.

I spaced my drinks so I was halfway through the second when the phone rang a little after six P.M. It was the desk clerk, who told me Mr. Wayland would like me to join him in the bar in five minutes time. As I walked out of my room, the door straight across the hall opened and Jackie Milne appeared. She was wearing the ultimate little black dress; clinging crepe with shoestring straps, cut square and real low in front so it revealed a deep swelling cleavage. The hemline stopped at mid-thigh, and the silver glitter stockings accentuated the elegant curves of her long legs.

"I'm late, already!" She gave me a quick smile, then took off down the hall in a gorgeous flurry of black and silver.

She got an elevator before me and by the time I reached the lobby she had vanished. For a moment there, I started to worry that maybe the gorgeous blonde was only a figment of my imagination, but then I happily remembered I can never imagine that good. When I walked into the Luau Bar I saw it was still doing good business with its fake Hawaiian drinks, served in an imitation coconut half-shell. I ordered a straight rye on the rocks and had time for the first sip before someone touched my arm.

"Hello, Boyd," a highpitched voice sneered. "Lost any more good fights lately?"

Ed Norman looked exactly the same as he had in Wayland's penthouse and that figured, because I didn't know of any reason why he should have aged overnight. Still the same tall skinny guy with thinning blond hair, and light blue eyes set too close either side of his thin pointed nose.

"I thought you were dead," I said in a surprised voice. "Died of a heart attack the moment after that butler pulled a gun on the assembled guests."

"If he'd been just ten seconds later, you'd still be limping from the beating George Thatcher would have given you," he snarled. "What the hell are you doing here in Santo Bahia?"

"Slumming, as of now," I said.

"You ask me, Stirling's gone clean out of his mind!" He sniffed loudly. "Who else, but some kind of a nut, would have set up that party last night, and make his guests listen to that crazy recording?" His light blue eyes stared at me balefully. "You know he's been missing for the last three days?"

"Have you told the police?" I asked softly.

Norman shrugged angrily. "After the things—the goddamned lies!—he told about me on that tape, I'm not interested in what could have happened to him. If somebody's murdered him already, I figure that's highly understandable!"

"I guess you'd have to fill in for him then?" I said. "Give your own advice to *Strategic Developments*, huh?"

"They might not take it," he snapped. "It was Stirling's name and reputation that made the board override Kurt Stanger in the first place."

"But you and George Thatcher being old buddies, and all?" I said easily. "He could swing it for you?"

"Do me one small favor, Boyd?" he whispered. "The moment after you finish your drink—drop dead!"

He turned and walked out of the bar quickly, leaving me to finish my drink in comparative peace. By the time I was halfway through my second drink it was a quarter of seven, and I was beginning to wonder if Stirling Wayland would ever show. Then I saw a familiar figure edging his way through the crowded drinkers toward me. He had a chameleon-like face, I figured, and that was why I'd had trouble trying to remember it the previous night. His face had looked like it belonged to a butler then, and now it suited a playboy out on the town.

"Hi!" He grinned broadly as he came up beside me. "Remember me?"

"Sure," I said, "but Chuck MacKenzie you're not, because I spoke with the real Chuck MacKenzie a couple of hours back."

"Is that right?" It obviously didn't faze him any. "Well, why don't you keep right on calling me, Chuck, anyway? That way, neither of us will get confused."

"Okay," I said. "What are you drinking?"

"Nothing. Stirling figured this might be too public a place to talk, so he asked me to pick you up and take you to him."

"Where is he now, Catalina Island?" I grunted.

"You've got a nasty suspicious mind, Danny!" he chuckled. "He's waiting for us out on the development. Nobody ever goes there anymore, because they don't want to be reminded it's a disaster area! A fifteen-minute drive, is all."

"I'll be real happy to meet him," I said, after I had finished my drink. "I was starting to wonder if Stirling Wayland ever existed."

"He's for real," the guy who wasn't Chuck MacKenzie said. "You'll find out!"

We drove north out of town, following the coastline for maybe five miles, then made a righthand turn onto a brand new pavement that abruptly became a dirt track a quarter-mile later. After a minute of bouncing along the humps, we went over an obviously brand new bridge, and "Chuck" pulled the car to a stop just the other side of it. Then he switched on the interior lights inside the car and relaxed in his seat.

"We're now sitting right in the middle of the graveyard of Kurt Stanger's dreams," he said. "The only thing a man needs more than a good idea, is the money to see it through." His index finger suddenly pointed toward the windshield. "Is that Stirling now?"

I looked out the windshield and couldn't see anything in the fast-gathering dusk. "I don't see anybody," I told him, and the next moment found myself staring down the barrel of a gun held less than six inches away from my face.

"Stirling figures I'm even more coldblooded than he is," Chuck said softly, "that's why he asked me to keep his appointment for him. He wants a couple of good answers to a couple of real good questions, Danny, and if I don't get them—you're dead!"

Chapter
FOUR

He wasn't kidding, I knew instinctively, and got that cold empty feeling in the pit of my stomach. It took one hell of an effort to look beyond the gunbarrel, and maybe that was another mistake. His face was set in a cold implacable mask, and the faint gleam in his hooded eyes said maybe he liked the idea of putting a slug through my head.

"I'm impressed," I told him, and my voice sounded real carefree, like it belonged to a mortician. "So ask the questions."

"Why did you murder Alysia Ames last night?" he asked in a clipped voice. "And what have you done with the tape recording?"

"I didn't kill her," I told him.

The gunbarrel moved a couple of inches closer and I went crosseyed trying to keep track of it. "You were the wrong man from the start, Boyd," he said. "I had to break my cover to stop Thatcher trampling all over you and destroying the tape. Then you had to try and get smart. Who got to you that quick last night?"

"Alysia Ames," I muttered.

"You can do better than that!"

"It's true." I told him the story of how she had come to my apartment and how, finally, she had walked out with both the recording and my gun, but had left her purse behind. Then afterward, I had gone to her apartment, let myself in and found her dead.

"The tape?"

"It wasn't there," I said. "I figured whoever had killed her, had taken it with them when they left."

"How about your gun?"

"It was there, on the floor."

"The murder weapon?" He groaned when I nodded. "You're in the wrong line of work, Boyd, you should buy yourself a shoe-shine kit and start over!"

"I'll consider it," I said, with an effort. "If Wayland— or you—had thought about briefing me in the first place, maybe things wouldn't have worked out the way they did."

"I hate to hear a grown man cry!" The sneering contempt in his voice made the bile rise in my throat. "You're all through, Boyd! Pack your bag when you get back to the hotel, and get the first plane back to New York. If I find out you're still in Santo Bahia tomorrow, I'll come looking for you with this gun! You've been paid a thousand bucks for the most complete foul-up I ever heard of, so figure yourself goddamned lucky to still be alive!" The gunbarrel moved back a couple of inches. "Now, get out of the car."

"What?" I stared at him.

"So it's an eight mile walk back to town," he grated. "Maybe the exercise will do that fat head of yours some good!"

Personal vanity is something that's never bothered me too much. I mean, with a profile like mine, who needs it? But in the last twenty-four hours I had been suckered all the way down the line. Thatcher beating the hell out of me, then Liz Ames pulling my own gun on me and walking out with that recording, and now finally the fake Chuck MacKenzie—having literally taken me for a ride —was about to put the ultimate polish on his character analysis by insisting I walk back to the hotel. The last fuse suddenly blew inside my head.

"Get out," he repeated impatiently.

"I'm going," I said plaintively, and opened the cardoor beside me. "Back over the bridge, follow the dirt track until I reach the new pavement, then that brings me out onto the highway, right?"

"Find out!" he snarled.

"Okay, okay!" I gave him a nervous placating grin. "One small favor, huh? I'm all out of cigarettes, just one right now would make all the difference."

"I was wrong about the shoe-shine kit—" he pushed

44

the gun inside his coat, then felt in his pocket for the cigarette pack "—you should be rattling a tin cup up and down Broadway!"

I slammed the edge of my hand across the apple of his throat and, while he was still making strangled grunting sounds, grabbed two handfuls of his hair then went backward out of the car, pulling him along with me. The moment my feet hit the ground, I pushed his head down fast and brought my knee up even faster. There was a dull ringing sound as my kneecap collided with his forehead, then his body suddenly became a dead weight. I let go my grip on his hair and he fell face forward onto the muddy ground.

His gun was on the floor of the car where he had dropped it when I chopped his throat, and the keys were still in the dash. I slipped the gun into my coat pocket, started the motor, then made a U-turn and headed back across the bridge. Maybe, I figured happily, the eight mile walk back to town would do that fat head of his some good.

Fifteen minutts later I parked the car and walked the one block back to the hotel, then went straight up to my room. The fake Chuck MacKenzie's gun was the same brand of Thirty-eight as my own, and it gave me an obvious idea. I tossed his gun into the bureau drawer, put my own back into my coat pocket, then returned to the car. After I had carefully wiped the gun clean of prints, I pushed it down the back of the driver's seat until only the end of the butt was showing. My fervent hope was he wouldn't realize he was carrying a murder weapon until sometime when it was too late, like when a ballistics department checked it out. Back at the hotel, I had a long leisurely dinner, and it was after ten P.M. when I got back to my room again.

I had a shower, shaved—there's no faster passion-killer than stubble rubbing against a girl's tender skin!—then got dressed in my West Coast native outfit. It consisted of a Prince Ferrari pearl gray shirt, tan slacks, a mint-colored silk sport coat, and a pair of tassel-fronted suede slip-ons, yet! Then I made myself a drink and saw I had another thirty minutes to wait before keeping my date with Jackie Milne. The phone rang a couple of minutes later and I answered it promptly.

"I'm going to kill you, Boyd," a dreadfully restrained voice said. "I just wanted you to know."

"Ah there, Chuck," I said affably. "Feeling healthy after the long walk back to town?" I waited until the choking noises had subsided before I continued. "If you're looking for your car it's parked a block down from the hotel, in Ocean Street. Your gun is tucked down the back of the front seat and—if you don't mind a word of advice?—why don't you invest in a shoeshine kit?" Then I hung up because he'd started making those choking noises again.

There was time for another mouthful of rye, then someone knocked on the door. A vision in black and silver smiled at me when I opened the door, and my tongue clove to the roof of my mouth at the sight of that magnificent deep swelling cleavage again.

"I got back early from my date, Danny," Jackie Milne said, "and I thought if you happened to be in your room, why don't we start our get-together now?"

"It's a great idea," I agreed. "After all, the sooner we finish our working day, the sooner we can start in on our private fun, right?"

She gave me a vague kind of smile then started back across the hall. I followed her into her room and she closed the door in back of us. Disenchantment set in the moment I saw the third person already comfortably installed in an armchair. The bourbon-colored hair was still stacked high in that elaborate cone, but now the blue eyes looked more fretful than stormy. She was wearing a wild

46

mini-dress, turquoise in color, spangled with huge white whorls, and a deep cut-out around her white navel.

"You remember Shari Wayland?" Jackie said.

"We met last night," I said, with no enthusiasm at all.

"Sit down, Danny," she said briskly. "I'll make you a drink while Shari tells you why she's here in Santo Bahia."

I sat down facing the bourbon-colored blonde and felt too dispirited to even bother watching the delightful bounce of the strawberry-blonde's bottom under the clinging black crepe, as she walked across to the bureau.

"It was in the New York afternoon papers," Shari Wayland said in a small voice. "I felt so scared after I'd read it, I didn't even stop to think! I just caught the first plane out here!" Her eyes widened as she stared at me. "Alysia Ames was murdered last night, Mr. Boyd. Shot through the head!"

I tried to look suitably surprised and shocked, so we both sat staring at each other until Jackie broke the hiatus by delivering my drink.

"I think this changes a lot of things, Danny," Jackie Milne said. "I know you're working for Stirling Wayland but—"

"Not anymore," I said. "I was fired tonight."

"You've seen Stirling tonight?" Shari asked anxiously.

"His butler, who isn't a butler but says he's Chuck MacKenzie, and MacKenzie he isn't, either," I explained.

The both of them stared at me blankly for a while, and I drank some of my drink while they figured it out.

"You mean," Shari ventured, "the new butler who was at Stirling's penthouse last night? The one with a gun who made us all leave?"

"Afterward, he said he was a personal friend of Wayland, who owed him a favor," I said. "Then he called me later and said he'd spoken with Wayland, and he wanted me to come out here. Tonight I was supposed to meet

47

Wayland in the bar, but he turned up instead and told me his name was MacKenzie. We drove out to the development, then he said I'd fouled up everything from the start —I was fired—and if I didn't get the first plane out tomorrow morning I'd be in big trouble."

The two blondes looked at each other for a long moment, then they both smiled slowly.

"Are you thinking what I'm thinking?" Jackie murmured.

"I could even be ahead of you, darling," Shari purred. "Maybe you'd better explain it?"

"It's like this, Danny," Jackie said. "Shari is petrified that whoever killed the Ames woman, may try to kill her. She wants protection—that's why she came here—but I'm no good at that kind of thing." She gave a brief self-deprecating laugh. "I doubt if I could even protect myself against any kind of physical attack! So now you're free of Stirling Wayland, will you take on the assignment?"

"Money isn't important, Mr.—I mean, Danny!" Shari gave me a dazzling smile. "I'll happily pay whatever Stirling was paying you."

"You mean, you want me to act as your personal bodyguard?" I queried.

"Exactly." Her fingers slid into the cut-out that encircled her white navel, and tugged the front of her dress down so the outline of her full breasts sprang into startling detail. "I'd be so grateful, Danny!"

"Why not?" I figured I had to find Liz Ames' murderer for my own sake anyway, and it would be no strain looking after the bourbon-blonde in the meantime. "But what makes you think whoever killed Alysia Ames will try and kill you?"

She shuddered delicately. "I can't explain it logically, it's just this horrible feeling I have that it's true. Now someone has murdered Stirling's mistress, I'm the only other woman in his life who's left. Maybe this does sound

48

crazy, Danny, but after all those wild lies Stirling told on that tape recording, I can't help feeling that he's behind the whole thing."

"You think he murdered Alysia Ames?"

"Or someone else did it for him," she said tightly.

"What motivation would he have for that?"

"Like I said before, I can't give you any logical reasons, Danny," she said, "it's just that I feel it—" her hand cupped her left breast tight "—here!"

"Maybe Danny and me can figure out a reason after we've matched our information," Jackie said smoothly. "You must be tired out after the flight and the worry, and everything, Shari. Why don't you go and get a good night's sleep?" She smiled at me. "Shari has the room right next door to mine."

"I guess you're right, darling." Shari got to her feet and stretched langourously. "Coming, Danny?"

"Huh?" I gurgled.

"Now you're my bodyguard I'm not going to let you out of my sight," she said determinedly. "I won't feel safe without you someplace close by me the whole time!"

"Darling," Jackie Milne said quickly, "you'll be in the next room. If anything happens, you only have to call out and Danny will come running to the rescue. And it is important we trade our information up to date!"

The murderous gleam in Shari Wayland's eyes slowly faded as she thought about that. "I guess you're right," she said finally. "Only don't keep Danny too long, will you? I want my bodyguard to be alert and eager at all times." She gave me a dazzling smile. "Your room is right across the hall, isn't it?"

"Sure," I nodded, "seven-two-eight."

"I just want to be sure, if I suddenly get scared in the middle of the night, I don't rush into the wrong room," she confided.

"You don't have to worry about that," Jackie said tartly, "I'm right next door to you, remember?"

"Of course, darling." Shari gave her a quick smile as she headed toward the door. "But I wouldn't dream of disturbing your beauty sleep. I mean, I know just how badly you need it!"

The door closed behind her and there was a short murder-impregnated silence.

"It's a funny thing," Jackie said in a strained voice. "But I'd forgotten that Shari is about the biggest bitch of all time!"

"That cut-out in her dress was real intriguing," I said conversationally. "I kept on wondering what would happen if I dropped a silver dollar into it?"

"You don't need money where Shari is concerned," she snapped. "Just your youth, and the kind of profile nature's given you."

"So why don't we start in matching our information?" I suggested tactfully.

"All right." She sat down in the chair Shari had vacated, and crossed her glittering legs. "You know about the set-up with *Strategic Developments?*"

"Some," I said. "They've overstretched themselves on this island development so they're now in big financial trouble. Thatcher managed to persuade their board to call in Wayland as a consultant, against Kurt Stanger's wishes. The hot tip is Wayland will suggest a merger which will freeze Stanger out entirely."

Her eyebrows lifted a fraction. "You're smarter than I thought, Danny! What else?"

"Wayland's recorded crack about Thatcher and Norman conniving together in their own interests against him. Stanger and Thatcher went to New York in a last ditch attempt—from Stanger's viewpoint, anyway—to raise some finance, and failed."

"It took me a couple of hours solid listening tonight to

50

get that far," she said. "Then I got a little further, but I don't see how it can help us."

"Like how much further?"

"You remember I told you about Alysia meeting Wayland after she had been divorced from Charles MacKenzie?"

"Sure," I said. "He tossed her out into the snow after he caught her having fun and games with four athletes, yet!"

"Most of the construction work for *Strategic* has been done by his outfit, and now he's their biggest creditor by a long way. From what I heard tonight, if he doesn't get paid off very soon he'll go broke."

"That's tough for him," I shrugged.

"This mystery man who played butler last night, and is working so close with Wayland," she said slowly. "I keep wondering why he used MacKenzie's name?"

"Maybe just to confuse me? One phony name is as good as another, right?"

"I guess so." She didn't sound convinced. "I'd go along with you more happily, Danny, if the Ames woman hadn't been murdered last night."

"The butler could have done it!" My grin faded the next second. "Alysia was MacKenzie's ex-wife who became Wayland's mistress, you mean?"

"It takes a little time," she murmured, "but finally the thought has penetrated!"

"So where's the connection between Wayland and MacKenzie, apart from Alysia?" I growled. "It figures MacKenzie didn't give a goddam what happened to his wife from the moment he threw her out of the house."

"Agreed," she said briskly. "But I think we should probe a little further and find out for sure if there is any other kind of connection between the two of them?"

"How do you suggest we start?"

"I'll scout around the business people my contact here

51

can put me onto," she said. "Then why don't you visit with MacKenzie in the morning? You can tell him you're still working for Wayland whose life has been threatened, and now that his ex-wife has been murdered—you know?"

"You're going to be the undercover brains of this partnership, and leave me to do the legwork?" I asked coldly.

"But there will be definite compensations," she said softly, "fringe benefits, and the like."

"Like what?"

"Like, would you like another drink?"

"Like I would," I said, "and like maybe you could call that some kind of compensation, but it's no fringe benefit."

She took the empty glass out of my hand, crossed to the bureau, and made a fresh drink. "Well," she said, with her back toward me, "I guess our working day is all shot now?"

"Not mine," I told her in a real casual voice. "I just got me a new job as a bodyguard, remember?"

Her back went rigid. "It's a kind of bad joke, isn't it? With me in the next room and you right across the hall, Shari only has to hiccup loudly to bring the both of us running."

"For me, she doesn't have to hiccup, even," I said simply.

She turned around with the fresh drink held in one hand, and gave me a long brooding look. Then she deliberately spread her fingers so the glass dropped onto the rug, and spilled good liquor in an ever-widening stain.

"How careless of me!" she said in a brittle voice. "I seem to have dropped your glass, and that was the last of the good stuff, too!"

"Don't worry about it." I gave her an amiable grin. "I guess it was time I started work, anyway. Check up on how Shari is making out all alone in her room. Maybe she needs help with a zipper, or something?"

The sapphire eyes fixed me with a long unblinking stare, while her teeth sank slowly and painfully into her full lower lip. Then she took a slow deep breath and obviously forced herself to relax.

"I'm glad you mentioned zippers, Danny," she said airily. "I'm having hell's own trouble with this one. If you wouldn't mind helping out before you start the night shift?"

She turned her back on me and waited expectantly. I got out of the chair and walked over to where she was standing, then ran the zipper down from her neck to the hollow just below her waist.

"Thank you, Danny," she said politely.

"Just common courtesy," I told her, "like helping a little old lady cross the street."

That fixed smile was back on her face when she turned around toward me, and shrugged her shoulders. The shoestring straps slid down her upper arms, then the little black dress just dissolved into a little black heap around her ankles. A lowcut cobalt-blue bra held her deep, widely-spaced breasts in a kind of nervous clutch, while matching briefs straddled her hips in a close embrace. The silver glitter stockings were supported by fancy black garters that bisected a fascinating four inches of bare bronze thigh.

"I knew I recognized you from someplace," I said solemnly. "You're the girl who fell out of the gatefold the last time I opened a man's magazine!"

"It's so hot in here!" Her voice had a childlike innocence. "Do you think there's something wrong with the air conditioning, Danny?"

"Could be?" I said. "I'm finding it kind of hard to breathe in here myself."

"Imagine what it would be like if you were wearing a

bra—like me?" Her hands disappeared behind her back a moment later. "I guess there's an easy way to fix it."

The practised shrug of her shoulders sent the bra straps sliding down her upper arms, and I watched the cobalt-blue flutter down to the floor like a flag of surrender. She cupped her beautiful breasts in both hands and squeezed them gently, extruding the coral peaks as they puckered in the cool air from the lousy air-conditioning plant.

"You're not trying to seduce me from my new job, or anything?" I asked anxiously. "I mean, you wouldn't want me to get fired before I've even started?"

"I wouldn't dream of doing a miserable thing like that to you, Danny," she said softly. "But if you're not in a hurry to start work right at this moment, I've just remembered there is another bottle of the good stuff on the bureau." She sat down facing me, crossed one glittering silver leg over the other without hurrying, then began to unfasten her garters, "You could make me one while you're at it."

I went over to the bureau, made two drinks real fast, turned around and found she had vanished.

"In here," her voice called from the bedroom, and a pair of cobalt-blue briefs sailed through the open doorway to give me a helpful hint.

She was stretched out on the bed with her hands clasped behind her head, the two narrow strips of white making a fascinating contrast with the rest of her all-over tan. I gave her the drink and she smiled vaguely over the rim of the glass at me, then took a long deep swallow of rye.

"You know something?" I said. "I think you were right all along about Shari. What the hell has she got to worry about when you're right here in the next room?"

"You don't think she needs a personal bodyguard within reaching distance the whole time?" she murmured.

54

"Damned right she doesn't!" I agreed.

"You mean I have seduced you from your new job?"

"Oh, yes," I sighed deeply. "Yes, indeed!"

"I'm so glad." She pulled the covers down with her free hand, jack-knifed her legs under them, then pulled them up until they covered her shoulders. "Goodnight, Danny."

"Huh?" I muttered.

"You can finish your drink on your way out." She thrust her glass at me and I took it in an automatic reflex. "Come to think of it, you can finish mine, too."

"Where did everybody go?" I asked desperately. "And I do mean that beautiful naked blonde in particular!"

"It was a challenge," she said evenly. "Shari started it, and then you kept pushing it, so I had to find out for sure."

"I don't know what the hell you're talking about!" I snarled.

"If I still had that old seduction bit still going for me." Her lips curved into a complacent, and hideously triumphant, smile. "I guess I still do?"

"You know something?" I grated. "I never seriously contemplated rape until this moment."

"Contemplating is as far as you'll get," she said confidently. "You'll never make a rapist, Danny."

"Don't bet on it!" I yelled.

"It's got nothing to do with any inherent decency or respect for the feminine sex," she went on in the same confident tone of voice. "No man with your colossal personal conceit could ever force himself on a girl who rejected him." Her lilting laugh was a revolting sound. "Your great vanity would never allow it!"

I finished my own drink in two large gulps, and hers in three. Jackie Milne let out a long and very audible yawn, turned over into her side with her back toward me, and closed her eyes. Every muscle in my body was uptight as

55

I walked back into the living room, deposited the empty glasses on top of the bureau, then headed toward the door.

Chapter
FIVE

Back in my room I made myself a giant-sized rye on the rocks, figuring that enough alcohol would finally obliterate the sexual frustration that still had my nerve-ends quivering like the strings of a bass fiddle. Then, a couple of minutes later, I heard a soft tap on the door. Blind unreasoning lust said it had to be the naked blonde lady who lived right across the hall, come to fall at my feet and plead for my forgiveness, because she'd just come to her senses and realized she was crazy for me. My cold-blooded desire for self-survival said it was the fake Chuck MacKenzie, come to carry out his already stated intention of killing me.

I lifted the Thirty-eight out of the bureau drawer, held it with the heel of my right hand pressed tight against my solar plexus, and stood carefully to one side before I suddenly pulled the door wide open. A blurred figure hurtled into the room then came to a sudden stop, and I saw blue eyes widening with terror as they stared at the gun in my hand.

"Don't shoot, Danny," she wailed. "I'll pay you double whatever Stirling promised for killing me!"

"Ah, shut up!" I said disgustedly, and used my foot to close the door. "You could have been anybody, and including Alysia Ames' murderer, right?"

A small tremulous smile crept onto Shari Wayland's

face after I returned the gun to the bureau drawer. She was wearing a black silk robe, I noticed, belted tight at the waist and just reaching the middle of her thighs. Her bourbon-colored hair had been brushed out so now it draped gently over her shoulders, and softened the strong planes of her face.

"It was seeing that gun in your hand," she said in a quavering voice. "I was so scared, I nearly died!"

"Maybe you can use a drink?" I suggested.

She nodded vigorously. "Don't dilute it with anything, either!"

I made the drink and gave it to her, then she collapsed into the nearest armchair. The neat rye disappeared so fast, it was like watching a conjuring trick.

"I just couldn't stand being all alone in that room any longer," she murmured.

"So you figured you needed your bodyguard within grabbing distance?" I said.

She nodded. "You guessed it, Danny."

"And the chances of me being alone with Jackie Milne for the rest of the night had nothing to do with it?" I prodded.

"Are you crazy?" Her voice had an incredulous sound. "No man in his right mind could prefer Jackie to me!"

"Whatever makes you think that?" I sneered.

Her blue eyes flashed storm signals, and her narrow top lip compressed tight over the full curve of her bottom lip, so her mouth set in a savage pout. Then she got up onto her feet, rested her clenched fists on her hips, and glared at me.

"I guess I didn't hear you right?" she purred. "So I'll say it one more time, real slow. No man in his right mind could prefer that limp eggheaded female to a woman who's all woman like me!"

"Why?" I snapped.

"I'll give you a small demonstration," she said tightly.

It was the same old routine all over again, I thought wearily as I watched her fingers release the belt around her waist, only this time it was a different blonde. There was a second difference also, I realized a second later; Jackie Milne had done a full strip from little black dress to cobalt-blue briefs, but Shari Wayland had no time for non-essentials. The robe fell open all the way down the front and, as she replaced her hands on her hips, it was like watching the curtain going up on a Broadway first night. Underneath the robe was just Shari, and it was one hell of an unveiling. Her body was sculpted with an abandoned generosity of curves, so her breasts had a pouter-pigeon plumpness, and her hips the swelling symmetry of an hour-glass. Her legs were maybe a trifle shorter than Jackie's, but they had the same elegant taper, I realized as I checked them all the way up from the delicate ankles to where they reached the bourbon-colored triangle.

"Cat got your tongue?" she asked in a mocking voice.

"So it's a female-type body," I said. "When you've seen one, you've seen them all."

Her mouth dropped open as she blinked at me maybe five or six times. "You mean," she stuttered, "you don't care if I spend the rest of the night here with you?"

"With a man and a woman it's just fine," I grated. "But when you get a man and two women, all he's got is trouble. Because then they start seeing him as trophy—a scalp they can hang from their belt to prove to the other woman that they're more attractive than she is. So why don't you belt up your robe real tight and get the hell out of here?"

"Danny?" The corners of her mouth drooped defenselessly. "You don't know what that profile did to me the first time I saw it, only then I thought you were with Alysia so I played it cool. From the moment you walked into Jackie's room, I've been planning a campaign that would end up with us in the same bed!"

58

"Big deal!" I snarled.

Her eyes flashed viciously. "I should have known! Those fruit boots you're wearing are a tip-off from the start. The trouble is these days, it's the goddamned fags who look more virile than most of the real men around!"

"You think I'm a fag?" I gurgled.

"Or worse, just impotent?" she sneered.

"Let me introduce myself," I said in a bright voice. "My name is Danny Boyd, and my profession, rapist!"

"I'd laugh, if it wasn't so pathetic," she snapped. "Delusions of manhood, I guess you call it?"

It was time for action, or the adrenalin pumping through my veins would start spurting out of my fingertips at any moment. I grabbed hold of her nearest wrist, twisted her arm up behind her back, then ran her across the room until her knees collided with the end of the bed. The moment before she fell face-down onto it, I let go of her wrist and grabbed a handful of the robe. It was like peeling a grape. I dropped the robe onto the floor and gave each gloriously-rounded cheek of her bottom a resounding slap—to prove I wasn't kidding—then quickly stripped off my clothes.

A long time later she lay on her back, the shaded bedlamp casting a warm glow across the milky whiteness of her body, and stared reflectively up at the ceiling.

"Would you like a drink?" I asked her.

"Why not?" she murmured.

I made two drinks and brought them back to the bed. She eased herself up into a sitting position and winced sharply as she took the glass.

"I don't bruise easy, but this time I'm going to bruise, for sure," she said. "Danny Boyd—rapist, huh?" There was a look of hotblooded approval in her blue eyes. "You know something? You're going to make a fortune in your new profession!"

"But where will I ever find another client as cooperative as you?" I asked.

"You'll never need another client, Danny," she chuckled lewdly. "I'm about to sign you to a lifetime contract."

The warm afterglow still permeated my body, and the rye tasted like some kind of nectar, but the curse of man is he's a thinking animal and now that passion was sated, my mind was starting to tick over again.

"How long have you been married to Wayland?"

"That sounds like some kind of a dirty crack, coming right at this moment," she said. "About five years, I guess."

"He's pure fantasy to me," I said truthfully. "In a little over twenty-four hours he's gotten me completely involved in a crazy deal that includes murder, and I've never even met the guy yet! What's he like?"

Shari shivered slightly, then poured the rest of her drink straight down her throat. "I never want to talk about Stirling," she said in a low voice. "But I guess my bodyguard should know what he's up against. He's forty-seven, built like a professional wrestler, and only the tiniest beginning of a potbelly. Almost all women fall for him at first sight; he's still got all his hair and just a touch of gray. Light brown eyes, and the kind of long lashes most of us dames have to buy at the beauty shop. It's the caveman appeal that makes even happily-married women a pushover for him. I felt the same thing when I first met him—under that smooth facade was a strong determined, completely masculine man!—but I didn't begin to appreciate his complete ruthlessness until after we were married. It was a little late then!"

She laughed, and there was a nervous edge to it. "Get me another drink, Danny?"

"Sure."

When I had made the fresh drinks and turned around from the bureau with the glasses in my hands, I saw she was sitting in an armchair with her robe belted tight around her waist again. She took the glass from me, then her lips twitched suddenly.

"Why don't you put some clothes on, Danny?" she purred. "You look ridiculous that way!"

"Thanks a bunch!" I snarled, and was dressed in a shirt and slacks in no time at all.

"It was irresistible," she half-apologized, "the same as me. Anyway, I figure it would be more tactful if I have breakfast in my own room, right?"

"I guess so," I agreed. "What happened between you and your husband?"

"The first couple of years weren't too bad, but after that, one thing was very clear. He didn't want a wife, he wanted a slave, and I wasn't about to submit to becoming his slave. For a while there he tried most every way to make me submit, including physical violence, but he finally realized he wasn't going to win so he quit trying. He moved me into another apartment, gave me a generous allowance, and said he was going to get himself a mistress. Enter Alysia Ames from stage left!"

"He didn't want a divorce?"

Her mouth twisted bitterly. "You heard what he said about that last night!"

"I also heard him say he had some kind of a hold over you, so you could never divorce him," I said. "Is that true?"

"It's true, and we'll leave that discussion right there," she said icily. "I don't know what the hell Stirling is hatching right now and I wouldn't give a goddamn, except for Alysia being murdered."

"You figure he killed her?"

"He'd be capable of it." She shrugged impatiently. "And if he didn't do it, he's very likely to suspect me. That's why I got Jackie up here from L.A. to see if she could find out exactly what was going on."

61

"But you called her a while before you knew about Alysia Ames?"

"That whole deal with the tape recording was enough to make me nervous! I've never known Stirling to take all that trouble before." She tried to laugh and didn't make it. "I even had the crazy idea he might be contemplating suicide, and fake it so it looked like I had murdered him. He's the most conniving bastard in the whole world, and he can hate like you never dreamed it would be possible for one human being to hate another!"

"Jackie Milne is an old friend of yours?"

"Since college," she agreed. "She's bright, too, and works for a real bright outfit."

"She told me the story of how Ames came to divorce her," I said. "How did you come to hear the story?"

"From Stirling, who else? He thought it was amusing, and it was also his way of letting me know he preferred any kind of a slut to me." She stared down at her glass like it was some kind of a crystal ball. "I don't understand the in-fighting between him and Stanger, and the rest of them. One thing I do know is that Stirling always has an angle—a special kind of angle that comes in from left field and people never know what hit them until it's too late—and there was a special kind of angle to that party where he played host on a tape recorder." She shook her head quickly. "I'm not making any kind of sense am I, Danny?"

"I don't know," I shrugged. "Maybe you're making very good sense. Tell me about Ed Norman. You think Wayland was telling the truth about him and Alysia playing house together when he wasn't around?"

"It's possible." She yawned widely, then grinned at me. "Sorry! I didn't realize just how tired I am, but then a girl doesn't get raped every night of the week." Her forehead knit in concentration. "Alysia would have slept with the

62

bellhop if she was in the mood, so why not Ed Norman? You saw him last night, Danny; he looks like the kind of fish you throw back because the thought of eating it turns your stomach. I always figured he was completely under Stirling's thumb and always did like he was told. But who knows what goes on in back of that repulsive face?"

"You're sure it was Stirling's voice on that tape?"

"I'm sure," she said flatly. "I lived too long with the sound of it, Danny. It was dear Stirling's voice, all right."

"The idea of hiring me as a bodyguard was just a gag?" I said. "You and Jackie had something planned for me before I ever walked into her room, right?"

"You were the enemy working for Stirling." She grinned widely. "We figured on using a little feminine strategy to see what we could get out of you, but then you told us you'd been fired before we'd even gotten started. So hiring you for our team was too good a chance to miss." Her voice sobered abruptly. "I don't think I need a bodyguard while I'm staying in this hotel, but I do want you to work with Jackie until we've found out what Stirling is about, exactly. It's the only kind of insurance I can buy against what happened to Alysia not happening to me, Danny!"

"It's fine by me," I told her.

"So—" her voice was bland "—you cooperate with Jackie, and you sleep with me."

"Is that a client's directive to the hired help?" I asked in a bleak voice.

"Just a hopeful suggestion, Danny, is all." She got out of the chair and yawned again. "I'm sorry, but I'll have to go to bed now or I'll fall asleep right here."

"Goodnight, Shari," I said.

She looked at me for a long moment with her blue eyes glowing, then threw her arms around my neck and kissed me like there was no tomorrow. "Thank you, Danny," she murmured, taking time out from nuzzling my neck.

63

"It's been so long, I'd almost forgotten what sex is all about."

"You could have fooled me," I said sincerely.

"I guess it's like learning to ride a bike?" She gave a short wanton-type chuckle. "Once learned, never forgotten!" Her arms unwound from around my neck and she backed off toward the door. "Sleep tight, Danny." Her eyes rolled expressively. "Is there any other way?"

"What kind of a hold, Shari?" I asked softly.

"You don't give up easy, do you?" She leaned her back against the door and her shoulders sagged a little. "I told you before, it's none of your goddamned business."

"For your own sake," I persisted, "I have to know."

"It's hard to remember there was a time when I wasn't Shari Wayland," she said in a tired voice. "The time when I was like carefree and single, and called Shari Ames."

"Related to Alysia?"

"My kid sister, a couple of years younger than me. I told her she was stupid to even think of marrying MacKenzie, a man who was thirty years older than her and had been married twice before."

"She must have been out of her mind," I said.

"No!" Her voice was suddenly vehement. "You never said anything like that to Alysia. She spent a whole year in a sanatorium when she was nineteen. The doctors said it was a nervous breakdown, but everybody else figured they were just using a polite phrase. After that, nobody tried too hard to thwart her will when she had her mind set on something, like marrying MacKenzie." She shook her head blindly. "I made the dreadful mistake of telling Stirling the whole story in the early days of our marriage, because I thought he'd be sympathetic. Even asked him to help me keep an eye on her. My God! He kept tabs on her like she was some kind of a blue chip investment. Guess who was there the day after MacKenzie threw her

64

out of the house, to offer consolation and a definite proposition!"

"So if you tried to divorce Wayland, you had to cite your own sister as the correspondent?"

"MacKenzie was decent enough to let Alysia get a divorce on the grounds of mental cruelty. Stirling threatened that if I ever tried to divorce him, he'd make sure Alysia's whole history was brought out in the courtroom— her mental instability—the reason for her divorce from MacKenzie—everything! That would mean the newspapers would get the whole story, too."

A kind of haunted look came into her eyes. "She just couldn't have stood up to it, her mind would have snapped. It would have been condemning her to spend the rest of her life in a sanatorium. I couldn't do that to anybody—" her voice faltered "—especially my own sister!"

"But now she's dead," I said mildly, "there's nothing to stop you from divorcing him?"

"All I need is the courage to try. You don't know Stirling the way I do, Danny. His great passion is to rule other people's lives completely, to make them his slaves. Up until now he's had two female slaves held tight under his thumb. Then suddenly, last night, he lost one forever. You think he's about to ever let go of the remaining one, Danny?"

Chapter
SIX

Charles MacKenzie was a big hunk of man, in his late fifties, with the kind of battered face you can bet will still be around long after all the beautiful people have vanished. He looked the right kind of guy to head up a construction outfit. Sun and wind had carved deep lines into his skin, given it a permanent rich mahogany color, and stamped crow's-feet at the outer corners of his shrewd gray eyes. He sat in back of a desk that was even more battered than his face, a massive cigar held between his stubby fingers, and took time out to study my face intently before he spoke.

"Boyd?" His voice was harsh. "A private detective from New York, investigating the murder of my ex-wife?"

"That's right, Mr. MacKenzie," I said.

"I figured there was something familiar about the voice," he grinned. "Sometime late yesterday afternoon you were a private detective called Milne, hoping I'd give you a lead as to where you might find her, right?"

"Right," I agreed. "I'd only just heard about you then, and I wanted to check you were real, not a figment of somebody else's imagination."

"You satisfied now?" he barked.

"You're for real," I acknowledged, "and you can be a big help to me, if you will?"

"Spell it out for me, son," he grunted. "Then I'll make up my mind about helping."

I kept it down to the essentials. Wayland had hired me

because he thought someone was trying to kill him. One of five people; his wife, mistress, partner, Stanger, or Thatcher. Then Alysia had been murdered the night before last, and Shari Wayland had come to Santo Bahia because she was scared she could be next on the list. Last night I had word from Wayland that I was fired, and his wife had hired me to try and find out who had killed her sister. She had told me most all of Alysia's background, the real reason he had divorced her, and her history of mental instability. I knew Wayland had been brought in as a consultant to *Strategic* against Stanger's wishes, and with the connivance of Thatcher. I also knew he had done most of the construction work for the development company and was their major debtor.

He puffed his cigar for a while after I had finished talking, the shrewd gray eyes busy computing everything and giving away nothing.

"You know about as much as I do," he said finally. "I'll help, if I can, if for no other reason than I don't believe in anybody getting away with murder. But I'm not sure I know anything you don't."

"The way I hear it," I said, "just about everything went wrong with the island development from the start. They hit rock where they didn't expect to find rock. The county reneged on their previous agreement about one bridge across to the island and insisted on three and Stanger's outfit ran out of money with the project only half-complete."

"You heard right." The harshness was back in his voice. "I personally fired a couple of previously-competent surveyors who should have found that rock, but didn't for some strange reason. Somebody got to City Hall and made them change that one bridge into three. I guess the record rainfall at the wrong time was the only kind of natural bad luck we got!"

"How come you got in so deep with Stanger?" I asked.

"It was the biggest local development ever planned, and I'm the biggest constructor around here, so it was a natural tie-in. Like always, I was the last guy to find out *Strategic* was in big financial trouble!" He rubbed the back of his hand slowly across his mouth. "It's no secret that, unless they get some money from someplace, I'll be wiped out."

"You could bring suit against them."

He laughed derisively. "They wouldn't have enough money to pay my attorneys' fees right now! My only hope is Wayland comes up with another one of his real smart corporate parleys and gets them onto a financial basis again."

"Has he talked with you about the situation?" I queried.

"Sure," he nodded. "He was in here maybe a week back, and spelled out just how desperate their situation was in words of one syllable. Then he suggested he could organize a merger between my outfit and theirs. The way he'd fix it, I'd come out as the guy with the controlling interest in the new company, and Stanger would be bounced so high he wouldn't come down until sometime next year. There was only one small problem: to swing it, I'd need to find somewhere around three million dollars cash. I told him he had a lousy sense of humor. He said maybe he could find somebody to lend me the money, and I said do that. I haven't seen him since."

"Nobody's seen him since," I said.

"You have," he growled. "How else did he fire you last night?"

"By proxy." I grinned at him. "His proxy was playing butler at his New York penthouse the night before last, but no butler ever buttled the way he did! Then he told me he was a friend of Wayland's who owed him a favor. His name was Chuck MacKenzie, he said."

The cigar was poised motionless in mid-air, halfway to-

68

ward his mouth, while the gray eyes stared at me with a savage concentration. "What did he look like?" he barked.

"He's got the kind of face that's hard to remember," I told him. "Someplace around thirty, I'd guess, and a real nasty streak of violence just below the surface."

"It sounds like Chuck MacKenzie," he snapped.

"Huh?" I goggled at him.

"For a guy who makes a living as a private detective, you're not real smart, Boyd," he growled. "You know how many times I've been married?"

"Three."

"I look like I'm impotent?"

"Oh, no!" I groaned. "It was so obvious I had to miss it completely. Your son?"

"Working with Wayland," he whispered. "Charles MacKenzie the second, my one and only son, and when he's dead I'll go spit on his grave!"

He pushed his chair back violently, then walked across to the window and stood staring out at the courtyard, with his back toward me. "My first wife took off with some foreign movie director, so I had the sole custody of Chuck from the time he was twelve years old. I tried just about every way I knew to get close to him, but I never could. His education was a kind of major disaster area, and by the time he was twenty I'd quit trying to find a college that would even look at him. For a couple of years there I tried real hard to teach him the construction business, but the only thing he ever learned was how to finagle the books, so he was cheating me for around a couple of hundred bucks a week when I finally caught up with him." MacKenzie was silent for what seemed a long time. "You heard why I divorced Alysia?" he growled.

"You came home unexpectedly and found some kind of a Roman orgy in progress," I said in a neutral voice. "Alysia, together with four athletic young men?"

"Three of them were Chuck's close buddies—" his shoulders hunched forward suddenly "—the fourth was Chuck himself."

I didn't say anything, because what the hell was there to say? He turned back from the window, his head wreathed in a cloud of cigar-smoke, and his lips stretched in a tight mirthless grin. "You heard I persuaded them to keep right on with what they were doing, and took some pictures?"

"I heard," I said.

"I told the other three to find someplace else to live, a long way from Santo Bahia, or I'd send prints of those pictures to where they'd hurt most. They had parents, employers, girlfriends—one even had a wife—and they got the point real fast. But my son deserved something special, I figured. So I gave him a beating. I'm good at that, learned it in a tough school! The kind of beating where you don't break anything, but it leaves the guy wishing you had, even a couple of weeks later. Then I went up to his room and destroyed everything he had, from his clothes to his personal record collection that was worth around a thousand bucks at the time. Finally I gave him a five dollar bill and told him to go seek his fortune someplace else than here. If I ever saw his face again I'd kill him, I said, and I meant every word, Boyd!"

"I'll believe it," I said.

"So what the hell is he doing back in Santo Bahia, and associated with Stirling Wayland?" He took two quick strides then smashed his fist down onto the desktop and the whole office jumped. "I heard he was mixed up in some dirty construction racket down San Diego way, a couple of years back, and only got out one jump ahead of the local sheriff. You know something, Boyd?" He glared savagely at me. "It's suddenly crystal clear who bought those two surveyors and a couple of votes down at City Hall about those bridges!"

70

"Maybe," I grated, "but don't go leaping into the saddle and calling out the posse just yet, Mr. MacKenzie. You don't have any proof that it was your son in back of the sabotage—if it was sabotage and not just bad luck—anymore than I have any proof he's working with Wayland. Until I see Wayland, I've only got your son's word that he's working with him and you've given me a pretty good idea what that's worth, already."

"You're right," he said reluctantly. "I've still got some influence around this town and I'll start asking some pointed questions as of now. Where are you at, Boyd?"

"The Ambassador hotel."

"I hear anything worthwhile, I'll call you," he grunted, "and you do the same, huh?"

"Sure." I stood up. "Thanks for your time, Mr. MacKenzie."

"Make it, Charlie." A slow grin split his battered face. "A couple of simple suckers like you and me should be on a first names basis, for our own protection!"

"It's Danny," I grinned back at him, "and you're right."

I stopped suddenly just as I reached the door and turned back for a moment. "I forgot to ask you one important question, Charlie."

"Right now I couldn't lend you a dime," he grunted.

"Have Stanger or Thatcher ever met your son?"

"Not that I know of," he said.

"How about Ed Norman, Wayland's junior partner?"

"The same answer. Why?"

"They were there in Wayland's penthouse the other night when Chuck was playing butler," I said. "It figures they didn't know him, if they didn't recognize him. The same goes for my client, Shari Wayland, I guess?"

"I never met her, not even in the eighteen months I was married to her sister," MacKenzie said.

"It leaves us with the one interesting question," I

71

thought out loud. "How come Alysia didn't recognize him? Or how come she pretended not to know him?"

"There's one thing for sure, Danny," he shrugged. "It's too late to ask her now!"

It was a ten-minute drive from MacKenzie's office to the offices of the *Strategic Development Corporation.* The limp blonde receptionist with the bad sinus trouble sniffed my name into a phone, then snuffled that Mr. Stanger would see me right away. A nervous look in her watery eyes said she had me figured as a process-server. Stanger's office was large, and had a look of faded elegance like the economy drive had started six months back, so nobody polished the desk anymore.

"Hello, Boyd," the human skeleton said in his reedy baritone. "You know, I'd just about convinced myself that you were part of a mental fantasy I'd concocted in New York, and now you have to show up in Santo Bahia!" His thin lips stretched a fraction, and I guessed it was about as close as he ever came to a smile. "I think it's most unfair of you!"

"Just about everybody seems to be here in Santo Bahia," I said easily, "including Shari Wayland and Ed Norman. The only exception is Alysia Ames."

"I heard about that," he said, and carefully cracked the knuckles of the first two fingers of his left hand. "A shocking tragedy! I imagine Stirling is distraught?"

"I wouldn't know," I told him. "I still haven't met him as yet. He fired me last night, via one of his associates, so I'm not real interested in how he feels."

"A man of sudden and bewildering decisions," Stanger pontificated idly. "If I may ask a direct question, Mr. Boyd? What keeps you in our beautiful city?"

"Shari Wayland. She's hired me to find out who killed the Ames girl."

"How interesting! And did Stirling demand the return of that strange tape recording when he terminated your services?" The speckled-brown eyes watched me carefully from under the shaggy black eyebrows as he waited for my answer.

"Maybe he forgot about it, what with the shock of hearing the Ames girl had been murdered, and all?" I suggested. "It's still in a safe place."

"I do admire your integrity, Mr. Boyd," he said in a hushed voice. "Most men in your position might well have decided to capitalize on the article in question, you know?"

"Like sell to the highest bidder?" I grinned at him. "It's a thought, Mr. Stanger. How much are you offering?"

He cracked another couple of knuckles while he carefully composed a rueful look on his face. "I'm afraid you know my present financial situation only too well at the moment, Mr. Boyd!" He wagged his head from side to side slowly, like an invisible metronome was giving him the beat. "I couldn't possibly manage more than five hundred dollars, and that would take a lot of finding." His head stopped wagging suddenly and he gave me a quick glance. "Cash, of course!"

"I'll keep it in mind," I said. "I still have to shop around the other interested parties. Maybe George Thatcher might up your bid?"

It took me a couple of seconds to realize the dry rustling sound, like old newspapers drifting in a breeze, was Stanger laughing. "I find that a fascinating thought, Mr. Boyd. Why don't we find out?" He stabbed a button on his intercom, and a tinny voice answered a few seconds later. "Come into my office, George, right away," he said almost gleefully. "I have an old friend of yours with me, who's dying to see you again." His spatulate index finger released the button again. "Right at this moment I can't make up my mind which one of us is being devious, Mr. Boyd." He leaned forward in his chair with his shoulders

73

hunched, and carefully laced his fingers together. "But we shall see!"

Thatcher came into the office a little time later, and stopped short with a look of surprise on his face when he saw me. Then his brilliant white teeth flashed as he grinned derisively. He still looked the same kind of rugged but definitely-right kind of executive image, to make any Madison Avenue advertising tycoon drool into his Napoleon brandy.

"Well! If it isn't the heavyweight champ of Sutton Place!" He chuckled nastily. "You're taking a hell of a chance, aren't you, Boyd? I mean, walking around without that tame butler to back you up with his gun if things look like they're getting rough?"

"You've got a strong sense of humor, George," I said mildly. "I took a quick look around that development last night and I've got to hand it to you, that's the biggest laugh I've ever had!"

"I do hate listening to grown men behaving like spoiled children," Stanger said. "Let us come to the point!" He looked up at Thatcher with an expressionless face. "Mr. Boyd has just informed me that Wayland fired him last night. He is now working for Mrs. Wayland, hired to try and find out who murdered the Ames woman."

"She would have spent her money better with a fortune-teller," Thatcher sneered.

"What concerns us, George, is that Mr. Boyd still has that tape recording and is prepared to sell to the highest bidder. I have offered five hundred dollars, but he expressed an interest in what you might be prepared to bid."

Thatcher ran one hand slowly through his wiry black hair, while he looked at me carefully. "It's a genuine offer?" he asked sharply. "There's still only the one original tape—no re-recordings?—a straight deal to the highest bidder?"

"That's how it is," I told him.

"A thousand bucks, cash," he said quickly.

"Which makes a combined offer from *Strategic* of fifteen hundred dollars in total, Mr. Boyd," Stanger murmured.

"Who the hell said this was a corporate bid?" Thatcher snarled at him.

"Thank you for clarifying the point for me, George," Stanger said in a gentle voice, then displayed his deep emotional reaction by cracking three knuckles in quick succession. "In fairness to Mr. Boyd, I think we should bring Ed Norman in here and give him a chance to make a bid. Go find him, will you?"

Thatcher hesitated for a moment and the scowl on his face said he was about to argue, then he turned on his heel and walked quickly out of the office. Stanger interlaced his fingers again and sat for a while, giving a remarkable impersonation of some kind of a corporate Buddha. I lit a cigarette, then leaned back in my chair and let the silence build.

"It's a jungle, Mr. Boyd," Stanger said in a whispering voice that sounded startlingly loud after the long silence. "I suppose that is the biggest cliché ever mouthed about the corporate world of big business? Yet it's taken me a little over thirty years to realize the absolute truth of the cliché. I find that quite remarkable!"

"I guess it must have occurred to you everything that's gone wrong with the development needn't necessarily all be just bad luck?" I said.

"You mean, industrial sabotage?" He nodded briefly. "I've thought about that very deeply, Mr. Boyd. But where is the proof?"

"It was just a thought," I muttered. "I hear tell Charlie MacKenzie's been exercising his mind along the same lines lately."

"Imminent destruction of everything you've fought for

years to build is an excellent mental stimulation," he said placidly. "I'm not surprised to hear Charlie's reaction has been the same."

"Tell me something, Mr. Stanger?" I asked abruptly. "You're a substantial stockholder in a corporation that's staring bankruptcy straight in the eye. The only thing that can save it is a merger and, like Wayland said on the tape, when that happens you'll be out on your ear. But at least your stockholding would still have value then. Isn't it a preferable alternative to the corporation going smash, so then you'll be left holding a whole bunch of worthless stock certificates?"

"You would be absolutely right, Mr. Boyd, if it were not for one thing," he said coldly. "Stirling Wayland is a shark. Any merger he organizes will neither be simple, nor what it appears to be on the surface. There will be certain—indefinites—shall we say? He will smoothtalk the board into ignoring them, until it's too late. The chances are that what first appeared as a simple merger between two parties, will finally emerge as a convoluted spiral involving four, or even more, corporations. And when that point is reached, one thing will be absolutely sure; that the original stock in *Strategic* will be just as valueless as it ever was!"

The door swung open and Thatcher came in, followed by Ed Norman, who still looked like the whole world was bugging him and he was about to freak out at any moment.

"Hello there, Ed," Stanger said brightly. "I imagine George has told you what this is all about?"

"Of course." Norman's light blue eyes filled with venom as he glared at me. "It would be pointless to question Boyd's ethics at this juncture, I imagine!"

"You know what it's like at an auction sale, Ed, old buddy?" I grinned at him nastily. "You put your money where your mouth is, or you button your lip!"

His fingers clenched involuntarily and his thin nose got an even more pointed look to it. "I understand the top bid is one thousand dollars?" he said in a stifled voice.

"Right," I told him.

"My advice is take it, Boyd." His mouth twisted into a triumphant grimace. "I'm not interested in bidding!"

"That's too bad." I got up from the chair and started toward the door. "Thank you for your time, gentlemen."

"Hold it, Boyd!" Thatcher snarled. "My bid was the highest, remember?"

"To date," I said over my shoulder. "There are a couple more interested parties I haven't gotten around to yet."

"Like who?" he bellowed.

"Why, George," I said reproachfully, "that just isn't a nice question. You should get your old college chum, Ed there, to bone you up on ethics. It could be a whole new experience for you."

Chapter
SEVEN

There was a note waiting for me at the desk when I got back to the hotel, which said to join Jackie Milne for lunch in the restaurant. She was waiting at a banquette in a corner alcove, sipping a martini, and looking superbly elegant in a white lace shirt dress. I slid onto the seat beside her and the waiter neatly trapped the both of us with a quick movement of the table. I ordered a seven-to-one martini with no fruit or vegetables, then gave the strawberry-blonde a bright sunny smile.

"You're looking very seductive again today, Jackie," I told her. "It must be getting to be a habit."

"Danny!" The sapphire color of her eyes darkened with some intense emotion. "About last night, I want to apologize to you! I don't know why I did it, but I do know now it was a cheap and nasty trick to play on you, and I'm truly sorry!"

"Forget it," I said. "Everything is strictly business between us from here on out." The waiter opportunely put the martini down in front of me and I lifted the glass. "Let's drink to a successful crime-busting partnership."

"Don't put me on," she said bitterly, "it's bad enough knowing how much you hate me!"

"I've been thinking of going into the rapist business on a professional basis—" I gave her another bright sunny smile "—and I want to thank you for the coaching you gave me last night."

She bit down firmly on her lower lip for a long moment. "If you don't stop it this moment," she said in a tremulous voice, "I'm going to bust our crying right in front of everybody, Danny!"

"That was something!" I sighed nostalgically. "The way you busted out of that little black dress, and then the cobalt-blue underwear. I swear, I was so excited I could have popped a shirt button at any moment!"

Her eyes closed tight, then she grabbed her drink with both hands and swallowed quickly until the glass was empty. Then she let out a great choking gasp and banged the glass back onto the tabletop. "If you'll excuse me?" she whispered. "I have to go now."

"Relax," I told her. "I was only kidding. Everything turned out just fine and dandy last night after I went back to my own room." I let a couple of seconds skid past then added, "Have you seen Shari today?"

Jackie nodded. "I thought she might have joined us for lunch, but when I looked in on her just a half-hour back

78

she was still in bed. She said she wasn't getting up before this evening, and something about being so completely exhausted after—" She looked at me with a sudden dawning suspicion in her eyes. "She didn't—I mean, you didn't?" Her jaw set hard. "You'll get yours, Danny Boyd!" she said in a murderous undertone. "Of all the sneaky lecherous lying bastards it's ever been my misfortune to know, you are—"

"I'm grateful to you, Jackie," I said with immense sincerity. "Without your help I would never have known that rape could be such fun."

For a moment there she looked like she was about to break off the nearest tableleg and split my skull with it, then her shoulders shook uncontrollably and she burst into helpless laughter. The waiter materialized beside the table, took one nervous look at the writhing Jackie, then thrust the menu-card into my hand and fled.

"It's a kind of poetic justice," she managed to say, between a whole series of explosive giggles. "The way things worked out, it made me some kind of a female pimp, setting you up for another woman! You think there's any kind of professional future in that, Danny?"

The thought was so hysterically funny, she dissolved into another spasm of manic laughter. I told the nervous waiter still hovering in the background to bring two servings of chicken hash, and a batch of fresh martinis. Jackie finally sobered down and wiped her eyes carefully.

"I'm glad it happened, now I don't feel guilty anymore." Her lower lip curled in a small pout. "Maybe just a little envious of Shari, but not guilty anymore." She sighed gently. "How was your morning?"

"Interesting, and confusing," I said truthfully. "And you?"

"Dull. Nobody could tell me anything we didn't know already." She shrugged briefly. "Maybe there isn't any more to tell?"

"I saw Charlie MacKenzie," I said, "and wondered out loud why a fake butler should call himself, Chuck MacKenzie, and got a real simple answer. The fake butler calls himself Chuck MacKenzie because that's his real name."

"You know something?" she confided. "I bet what you just said makes a lot of sense, but not to me!"

"Three times married," I growled, "and a son by the first marriage?"

"Oh?" she said, then, "Oh!" again.

"Exactly. To put it mildly, Charlie doesn't like his son at all. The last words he had with him were to the effect that if he ever saw him again, he'd kill him."

"I see," the strawberry-blonde said slowly, then just sat there trying to look intelligent.

"You don't see anything," I snarled. "Alysia and the son knew each other intimately. Well, you could say, so why did they pretend to be strangers in Wayland's penthouse the other night?"

Jackie waited until the waiter had served the fresh martinis, then gave me a cold glance. "You're just full of good questions, aren't you?" she snapped. "How the hell would I know why they didn't recognize each other that night?"

"There's one person who maybe has all the answers, and that's Wayland himself," I said. "And where the hell is he?"

"I refer you to my last statement," she grated.

"He's got to be in Santo Bahia because this is where his action is," I persisted. "If he leaves that merger hang much longer, the whole deal could blow up in his face."

"We could go ring doorbells this afternoon and ask?" she said bleakly. "You start one end of the town and I'll start the other, and we should meet up together in a couple of weeks from now."

"You're bringing out the rapist in me again," I warned her, "and it would look kind of stupid right here in the middle of the chicken hash, and all."

"You're right," she nodded solemnly, "and it would clash with my chartreuse-colored underwear." Her eyelids flickered briefly. "Thin silk, and almost completely transparent. I'd probably catch my death of cold."

I gargled frantically on a mouthful of martini then finally managed to swallow it.

"Something upset you, Danny?" she asked solicitiously.

The waiter served the chicken hash right then and somehow it didn't look right to me, like it was chartreuse-colored, but that was ridiculous! It was obvious we both had the same motivation—hunger—so the conversation died until we reached the coffee stage of the meal.

"I forgot one thing Charlie MacKenzie told me," I said. "He saw Wayland about a week back, who suggested a merger between Charlie's construction outfit and the development corporation. Wayland said he'd guarantee him a controlling interest and all it would take was around three million dollars. So Charlie asked where would he get that kind of money right now, and Wayland said maybe he could find somebody to lend it to him. Charlie said for him to do that, and hasn't seen Wayland since." I finished my coffee. "You make any sense out of that, partner?"

"Shut up," she said coolly, "I'm thinking."

"Who am I to ruin a whole new experience for you?" I snapped.

I drank another cup of coffee and smoked a cigarette while she just sat there with a rapt expression on her face. Maybe the waiter had slipped some pot into her chicken hash, or something? It got to the point where I couldn't stand it any longer, so I put my fingers under her nose and clicked them sharply.

"Father and son hate each other, and the son is working with Wayland, who proposes a merger between father and the development corporation," Jackie said in a hushed voice. "He knows father is about bankrupt because of money owed him by development corporation, therefore probably can't raise three thousand, never mind three million dollars! He also knows that construction engineer would be a mere child in the financial jungle where he is king!" Her eyes glowed excitedly as she flashed me a quick glance. "Put it another way—simple—so you can understand it, Danny? If Wayland finds him the money, he knows he can easily baffle construction engineer with complex merger to the point where MacKenzie is back where he started, except that he doesn't even own a bankrupt construction outfit anymore. Grant that hypothesis and there's only one place where Wayland would go to borrow the money, and that's from himself!"

"There's one thing I always say about the California climate," I ventured. "Out here you can grow more nuts to the square foot than anyplace else in the whole country. And talking of nuts—"

"Don't you see it, Danny?" she said excitedly. "Wayland goes to the board of *Strategic Developments,* and tells them MacKenzie has found a solid financial backer, and proposes a merger between them. The board will be so grateful, they'll toss Stanger out the nearest window, and tell Wayland to go ahead. After the merger is completed, because of some tricky clause Wayland has planted in the agreement, MacKenzie will suddenly discover the corporation who loaned him the money has the right to vary the repayment time, and if he can't meet the terms, it also has the right to foreclose on his interests in the merger. This corporation will only be a front for Wayland himself, of course!"

She shook her head impatiently. "It won't be quite as simple as that, I know! But Wayland's a pastmaster at this game. Some of the best corporate lawyers won't go up against him, because they say he's still inventing the rules of the game."

"You're not just smart," I said admiringly, "you're brilliant!"

"It's just because it's my line of work," she said modestly, while her face flushed a bright crimson with pleasure.

"And it explains why Chuck is working with Wayland," I added. "He'll get one hell of a kick out of watching his old man slide into the manhole, and disappear out of sight! Maybe he's even been helping the whole deal along from the start, with constructive sabotage of the development all along the line?"

"So," she said happily, "where does that leave us now, Danny?"

"Right back where we started," I snapped. "We have to find Stirling Wayland, and our big problem is where to start looking?"

"I can feel my chartreuse silk underwear wilting at the thought of trying to come up with an intelligent answer," she murmured.

"Are you female pimping again?" I demanded frostily. "Trying to set me up for a matinee with Shari?"

"Just checking," she said in an idle tone of voice. "You still twitch everytime I mention it, which shows I made some impact on you last night and—" she looked away from me across the room "—and who knows? Maybe Shari will sleep right through until tomorrow morning?"

"Let's get back to Wayland," I said determinedly. "There's one guy who knows where he is, and that's Chuck MacKenzie."

"If you figure he'll be any easier to find, I'm all for going out and looking for him first," she said.

"He promised to kill me last night," I told her. "So the chances are we won't have to go look for him at all, he'll come to me, instead."

"You're cute, Danny, you know it?" She smiled at me fondly. "What is it? Some little boy hero complex that makes you dream up wild stories like that?"

"It kind of satisfies the rapist in me, too," I grated. "Like my headshrinker is always telling me, never argue with a certain kind of dame because you'll find that underneath that sleek strawberry-blonde hair is nothing but a big empty vacuum!"

"Is that right?" She was busy watching the passing parade across the floor of the restaurant, and obviously hadn't heard a word I'd said.

"Damned right!" I warmed to my theme. "You can always tell the type, he says, because they have a vacant look in their sapphire-colored eyes and a cute little mole on the right cheek of their buttocks, mostly."

"I never knew that?" she murmured obliviously. "Danny?"

"He left five minutes back," I snarled. "There's a guy called Frankenstein in the kitchen and I'm real confused, because five minutes back I was nothing but leftover chicken hash!"

"Have you got any friends in Santo Bahia?" Her voice was suddenly interested.

"I've forgotten the meaning of the word," I said.

"They're heading right for our table, and I've never seen them before in my whole life." She giggled excitedly. "You figure they just flipped when they saw my breathtaking beauty and are on their way over to try and make a date?"

"Who?" I followed the direction of her fascinated gaze, and felt like I'd just been kicked in the stomach. "Fuzz!" I gurgled frantically.

"Well, sure, everybody has it?" Jackie frowned severely. "But I don't think it's a nice topic of conversation in a restaurant!"

"Cops!" I hissed. "Police, you numbskull!"

84

"Really?" She preened herself unconsciously. "How fascinating! I've never met a real live police officer socially before."

"What makes you think you're about to meet one socially now?" I moaned, and then it was too late.

They stopped beside the table, and the older of the two —the one that looked like he'd been weaned on high explosive—flashed his tin under my nose. "Mr. Boyd?" His voice sounded somehow reminiscent of a jackal in hot pursuit of its prey.

"This is Mr. Boyd," Jackie said brightly, before I even had a chance to tell them my name was Smith, and I owned an antique shop in Rocky Falls, Nevada. "I'm Jackie Milne," she confided in a sexy whisper which had absolutely no effect on the fuzz at all.

"Sergeant Donavan," the jackal-voiced guy said. "We'd like you to come with us, Mr. Boyd."

"Has he done something dreadful, Sergeant?" Jackie asked breathlessly.

He turned his head a full half-inch and stared coldly at her. "I wouldn't know, lady." His eyes took their time about dissecting her white lace shirt dress from the neck down to where it disappeared under the tabletop. "Maybe you can answer that question better than we can?"

"Uh!" Jackie swallowed hard, her face reddening, and her eyes furious, then tried again. "Uh!—uh?—uh!"

"Don't worry about it, Sergeant," I said, as I pushed the table back and got onto my feet. "It's just that her green chartreuse underwear is strangling her to death."

"*Uh!*" Jackie swallowed hard again, then her eyes rolled wildly and she started drumming her fist on the tabletop.

The sergeant watched her incuriously for a couple of seconds, then shrugged his shoulders. "It takes all kinds. I had an aunt who used to rush out into the backyard everytime it had been raining, and sprinkle salt over the worms. She figured it would make them tastier for the birds. Let's go, Boyd!"

We went out of the hotel to the car parked at the curb with a driver at the wheel. The other two gently organized me into the middle of the back seat, and sat either side of me. It was the kind of respect given by the fuzz only to guys whose crimes rated real big, and it didn't cheer me up at all.

"I know it's a stupid question," I said tentatively as the car pulled out into the traffic, "but what's this all about?"

"You'll find out," Donavan said, and that did the conversation up real good for the next twenty minutes.

There was a dirt track that looked like it was going no-place for the first couple of miles, then suddenly decided to climb straight up the edge of a canyon. At the top was a lone shack, and it must have been a big day for the owner because there were maybe six cars parked out front, including an ambulance. Donavan got out of the car and held the door open for me, while his partner came around the trunk, not moving real fast, but fast enough if I tried anything stupid. The group of uniformed fuzz moved back out of our way as we walked up onto the front porch, then through the open doorway inside the house.

I could tell right off it was the corpse sprawled on the floor that made the living room the focal point of interest. The body of a big man lay on its back, with his head to one side, and the area above his left ear was a blackened bloodied mess. I mentally checked out the description Shari had given me the previous night. In his late forties, built like a professional wrestler, a thick thatch of hair with only a tinge of gray, and the wide open eyes staring blindly at the far wall were a light brown color.

"You know who he is, Boyd?" Donavan asked.

"I never saw him in my whole life before," I said truthfully.

His partner started to laugh, but stopped suddenly when the sergeant looked at him. We stood in silence for what seemed a hell of a long time, and it looked like nobody was in a hurry to go anyplace, or do anything. I was beginning to wonder for just how long the Santo Bahia police force had been recruiting the flower children, when the sergeant spoke again.

"Name of Wayland—Stirling Wayland," he said. "Somebody put four slugs into his head at a range of about two feet. I figure they must have been feeling a little nervous at the time?" He jerked his head toward the door and repeated what I suspected was about to become a painfully-familiar phrase. "Let's go, Boyd!"

Chapter
EIGHT

Time had only emphasized the infinite repulsion of Lieutenant Schell's office, I saw as I walked through the doorway. The walls were the same attractive color of old dried blood, and the converted packing crate which pinch-hit as a visitor's chair looked more unstable than ever. The lieutenant himself was still the same tall, tough character with close-cropped gray hair, and his hooded dark eyes looked even more malignant than ever.

"Picked him up in the hotel restaurant, Lieutenant," Donavan said. "He'd just finished eating, and he had some crazy blonde for company."

"Figures," Schell said.

"We had a kind of small private wake out at the shack, with Wayland's body lying right there at our feet," the

87

sergeant continued. "Boyd figured he'd never even seen him in his whole life before."

"Thanks, Pete." Schell made a small gesture of dismissal with one hand and the sergeant went out of the office, closing the door carefully in back of him. "Sit down, Boyd." The lieutenant nodded toward the packing crate.

I sat down very carefully in case the whole damned thing disintegrated out from under me, and fumbled for my cigarette pack. "I'll say one thing, Lieutenant." I bared my teeth at him. "You're way ahead of any other police force in the whole country. Anyplace else the cops are the law, but here in Santo Bahia they're a goddamned law unto themselves!"

There was a vaguely baffled look in his hooded eyes as he stared at me silently. It didn't faze me any—taking three matches to light my cigarette was purely coincidental! He let the tension build to screaming point, then exhaled a gentle sigh.

"Just how long have you been out of your mind, Boyd?" His voice was almost sympathetic.

"What the hell is that supposed to mean?" I rasped.

"Why pick Santo Bahia—of all places!—to try and get away with murder?"

"You figure it was me who killed Wayland?"

"I know it," he said confidently. "With all the hell-raising you've done around this town in a couple of previous visits, you must have known we kept tabs on you from the time you checked into your hotel?"

"Sure, I knew it!" I stared at him blankly.

"You must have also known we've got a dossier on you—" he held his thumb and index finger a couple of inches apart "—that thick?"

"That, too," I agreed.

"Any information we didn't get from you, we got from New York." He shook his head briefly. "The kindest

88

thought is maybe you got slugged across the head some-time, and just haven't been the same since?"

"Maybe if you said something like a fact?" I snarled. "Then I could understand what the hell you're talking about."

"Why not?" He opened the top drawer of his desk, took out a gun, then slid it across the desktop toward me. "That's a gun," he said softly, "and that's a fact!"

My fingers closed over the butt of the Thirty-eight and started to lift it. Then I knew what it was all about, and it was like a streak of forked lightning hit the top of my head and burned all the way down to my feet.

"The murder weapon." Schell's voice sounded a couple of miles away right then. "Your gun, Boyd! The serial number checks out, I've got it all here on file."

I squeezed my eyes tight shut until the red haze of fury started to fade, then eased them open a slit at a time. "So my gun was used as a murder weapon," I said. "That automatically proves I'm a murderer?"

"Hell, no! I can understand you lost your gun, or maybe it was stolen?" His voice was gently cynical. "Too bad you were so busy at the time you forgot to report it, Boyd."

It was a murder weapon twice over, I remembered, and my stomach lurched like it had never even sighted the chicken hash. Sooner or later, somebody was going to match the slug they had taken out of Alysia Ames' head in New York, with the four slugs they would take out of Wayland's head in Santo Bahia. When that happened about the only choice I'd have left, would be between the gas chamber and the electric chair. I wculd have bust out crying right then, except Schell would have taken it as a sure sign of guilt.

"The gun is enough to book you on a first-degree homicide, and get an indictment!" He smiled affably. "You want some coffee?" I nodded and he rang through for it, then settled back comfortably in his chair after he'd hung up. "I'm sure you're going to see it my way, Boyd. You don't have any choice but tell me all about it, do you?" He waited expectantly for around ten seconds, then shrugged easily. "Take your time about deciding, there's no hurry. We've got the rest of the afternoon and if that isn't long enough, we've got the whole night ahead of us. I mean—" he pushed his point home with all the delicacy of a raging bull elephant "—neither of us is going anyplace, right?"

"Has the coroner established the time of death?" I asked.

"Between four and five A.M. this morning."

"I was in bed in my hotel at the time," I said.

"Alone?"

It couldn't have been later than three A.M. at most when Shari returned to her own room, I remembered bleakly, but right then I decided the fuzz had enough going for them already without any voluntary help from me.

"Not alone," I said.

"Hey, maybe that's a lucky break for you, Boyd!" His bonhomie was about as real as the color of Jackie Milne's hair, I figured. "So you've got some kind of an alibi, huh? And who was the lucky lady who shared your bed last night?"

"You know something?" I scowled at him. "This buddy-buddy bit makes me want to throw up! Why don't you revert to your usual repulsive and oafish self, because I like you better that way."

"So what was her name?" he snarled.

"I forget. You mind if I call my lawyer now?"

"I mind!" The edge of his hand chopped down across my wrist as I reached toward the phone. "And I'm not violating your constitutional rights, Boyd, I'd like you to know that." He grinned wolfishly. "It's just that the Santo

Bahia police department hasn't gotten around to recognizing the Constitution yet."

A uniformed cop brought in the coffee and it made for a small break in my misery. I didn't like the way Schell looked so goddamned comfortable in his chair, or the way he sipped his coffee with such obvious and leisurely enjoyment. Maybe he'd been telling the truth about being prepared to sit around the rest of the afternoon, and the whole night if neecssary, until I talked?

"I don't think you'll find any headshrinker who'll support the theory that I've lost my mind," I said carefully. "And of course I knew you had a dossier on me that thick, and any details you didn't get from me, you'd get from Center Street."

"So?" he grunted.

"So if I'd killed Wayland with my own gun, you figure I'd be that stupid to leave it there?"

"Maybe you got nervous?"

"Normally, I wouldn't dream of mentioning this, Lieutenant," I said modestly. "But you may recall last time I was here I shot a man dead—strictly in self-defense as you agreed!—and the time before that there was—"

"There's one hell of a difference between shooting somebody in self-defense, and murdering somebody in cold blood!"

"You believe I'd leave my own gun hanging around the scene of the crime, then I give up!" I grabbed the coffee pot and upended it over my empty cup, then watched five blobs of sludge slowly drip out of the spout.

"Don't worry about it," Schell said cheerfully. "We'll have another coffee break sometime around midnight, I guess?"

"Who found the body?"

"An anonymous tip-off. Somebody called in and refused to give their name."

"It was me," I said in a solemn voice. "I just wanted to

make sure you found the body before the serial number had rusted off my gun!"

His face darkened a little and I felt maybe I was beginning to get to him. "Don't try and get cute, Boyd!" he rasped.

"Ah, come on, Lieutenant!" I groaned. "That shack is to hell and gone in the great wide loneliness! Nobody in their right mind would ever go near it in a month of Sundays. But some anonymous explorer finds the hut inside twelve hours of the murder, and walks straight into the living room and finds the body. You figure he's got E.S.P., or something?"

He lunged out of his chair and yanked open the door. "Donavan!" he roared, and out Miami way they must have figured another hurricane was getting ready to rip. The sergeant appeared a few seconds later and Schell pointed his index finger at my chest.

"Put him in a cell someplace," he grated. "I'm getting sick of the sight of his face!"

"I haven't called my lawyer yet," I reminded him.

"We'll check out his number for you," he sneered. "What's his name again—Smith?"

"You haven't even booked me yet!" I yelled at him.

"Protective custody," he snapped. "It's not so bad, Boyd; whenever you get tired of lying down, you can always stand up for a while. Then, if you get tired of standing up, you can—"

"I have a special suggestion about what you can do, Lieutenant," I said carefully. "First you take your—"

Donavan's hand grabbed hold of my elbow and yanked me clean out of the lieutenant's office before I'd even gotten to the interesting part of my suggestion. It took all of thirty seconds for Donavan to hustle me into a cell, and the turnkey to lock me in. I guessed it was too late now to even think about changing my name to Diablo Bonanza, and head for the Argentine. Become a gaucho and go charging all over the Pampas, waving my boleros wildly above my head! Or was it the bolero who charged all over the Pampas, waving his gauchos wildly over his head? Right then, it seemed an academic kind of question.

An hour later I realized Schell had been right about the limited choice of physical activity inside a cell. Like he said, you could lie down, then for a change of pace, stand up. You could even walk a little if you took small steps and didn't mind reversing direction every three seconds. A couple of hours later I could still hear my mind gibbering gently to itself, which was kind of unnerving because it presumed a split-personality already. Then the turnkey clanked up to the door and unlocked it.

"Out, Boyd!" he boomed.

He didn't need to tell me twice. I shot out of the cell faster than a stripper who's just been goosed by a real live goose, then followed him through an intricate maze back to the lieutenant's office. Schell was lounging in the doorway, his hands thrust deep into his pants pockets, and the look on his face could only be described as enigmatic.

"The widow lady herself?" He shook his head slowly. "You surely get around, Boyd!"

"What is this?" I stared at him suspiciously. "Widdle-wound-up time?"

"A little advice," he said. "Don't try to leave town because if you do, I'll nail you to the nearest wall with a pattern of point three-eight slugs. Don't get into any trouble—and that does include jaywalking!—or I'll bounce you right back where you've just come from. Don't change your hotel without getting my permission first. There was something else." He stared at the flyspecked ceiling for a couple of seconds. "Now, I remember! Some other time when you're not real busy—like when you're serving your ninety-nine years in San Quentin—you must

93

tell me the secret of becoming a superman." He shook his head slowly. "My wife would sure appreciate that!"

I let all his doubletalk slide right by me and hung onto the one essential. "You mean you're letting me out of here?" I croaked.

"But not for long, I devoutly hope!" he grunted.

The moment I stepped out onto the sidewalk, the heady feeling of freedom hit me right between my eyes, and I would have walked right by the two blondes waiting there if they hadn't each taken one of my arms in a firm grasp, then steered me toward a parked car. Jackie Milne drove, with me sitting beside her, and Shari Wayland on my other side.

"You did it?" I looked from one to the other with my eyes bulging wildly. "You're magnificent! But—how?"

"Shari heard the news on the radio this afternoon about Stirling's body having been found in a lonely shack," Jackie said. "She came charging into my room and told me all about it, and when she said the police had already detained a man for questioning in connection with the murder, I guessed it had to be you."

"They said Stirling had been killed in the early hours of the morning," Shari said quietly. "My problem was—"

"Our problem, darling," Jackie corrected her firmly.

"Of course, darling!" Shari said apologetically. "Our problem was to figure out just how early in the early hours. As I remembered, it was sometime around three A.M. when I went back to my own room." Her voice suddenly developed a dreamy quality. "So beautifully and totally exhausted after all that wonderful—"

"No intimate details, darling," Jackie said, with a hard edge to her voice. "Leave us stay with the facts!"

"We had the feeling you could be in need of a very good alibi, indeed, Danny," Shari resumed her story in a no-nonsense kind of voice. "I mean, an alibi that quits cold at three in the morning, is no kind of alibi at all. So we decided that I'd tell the police I'd spent the whole night with you."

"It wasn't a perfect alibi, exactly, even then," Jackie said. "The widow of the murdered man giving the suspect that kind of sex alibi? You see how we felt, Danny?"

"I do," I said numbly. "I do, indeed! So how did you overcome the problem?"

"It was very simple, really," Jackie said in an elaborately-modest voice.

"Simple!" Shari squealed. "It was all Jackie's idea, and it was a stroke of genius!"

"We just doubled your alibi," Jackie murmured.

"That was good thinking, doubling it," I said. "What the hell do you mean?—doubled it!"

"Well—" Jackie cleared her throat cautiously "—even a suspicious-minded police officer would find it hard to believe any man who spent the night with two gorgeous blondes like us, would find either the time, or the inclination, to leap out of bed sometime in the early hours of the morning to go and commit a murder, wouldn't he?"

We traveled three blocks before I could get my voice to function again. "Did you tell that to Lieutenant Schell?" I asked slowly.

"Of course," Jackie said. "He seemed to be the top man around the place, so naturally we spoke with him."

"I think he'd be quite a nice man," Shari said in a benevolent voice, "if he wasn't a police officer, that is."

"What did he say?" I gurgled.

"Nothing," Jackie said flatly.

"I thought he was goddamned rude," Shari stated in a fierce voice. "The way he stood there and kept on staring at us for maybe five minutes, before he said anything!"

"Was anyone else around?" I prodded hopefully.

"That slob of a sergeant who insulted me in the restaurant," Jackie snapped, "and another two or three uniformed men."

"Did anybody say anything?"

"Not really." She hesitated for a moment. "Donavan did mutter something under his breath about, oh, his aching back, but I couldn't sympathize with somebody as crudely-mannered as he is!"

"Danny?" Shari said in an alarmed voice, maybe a minute later. "Are you sick?"

I managed to shake my head, but even that was almost too great an effort.

"I think he's got a fever, or something?" Shari persisted. "He's shaking like a leaf!"

"They probably gave him the third degree, or something equally bestial," Jackie said in an emotional voice. "The brutes!"

Maybe I could have contained it but at the last moment, just as I was about to step out of the car, Shari blew the whole bit.

"Jackie, darling," she said in a decisive voice, "I think the best thing we can do for poor Danny is put him straight to bed!"

I missed my step, pitched face-forward onto the sidewalk and wound up at the doorman's feet, screaming out loud with hysterical laughter. Later, in Jackie's room, even after I had profusely apologized for around ten minutes straight, they still didn't think it was the least bit funny at all.

Chapter
NINE

"I can't pretend I'm sorry Stirling is dead," Shari said. "All I feel is a tremendous sense of relief. That stupid lieutenant looked real shocked when I told him that!"

"I guess he asked a lot of questions?" I said.

"That's why you had to stay in a cell for so long," she explained. "I thought he'd never stop. Most of the time whenever I was telling him about something important, I'd catch him looking at me out of the corner of his eye like I was some kind of a nut!"

"Especially when you told him what happened in New York," Jackie agreed. "I noticed that, too. The way he reacted, you'd figure he'd never even heard of a tape recorder before."

"You told him about Alysia?" I asked, and tried to make it sound like a casual question.

"Of course," Shari nodded. "Absolutely everything, except that kind of private family thing I mentioned to you last night."

"It amazes me how a stupid man like that manages to hold down such a responsible job," Jackie said tightly. "I explained the whole theory of Stirling's merger-plan and how he could cheat Charlie MacKenzie out of everything finally—in absolute detail, the same way I did for you at lunch, Danny—and you know what?" She laughed bitterly. "He didn't even understand one word! He just looked at me in a kind of dazed fashion, then asked some idiot question about was I sure you hadn't arrived in Santo Bahia until the day after Alysia Ames had been murdered?"

"And you said?" I whimpered.

"Of course I was sure you didn't arrive until the day after," she said tartly. "I clearly remember Shari telling you it had been in the New York afternoon papers, and how you tried to look surprised and shocked for her sake."

"Is that the way you told it to Schell?" I asked in a petrified whisper.

97

"Exactly." She smiled brightly at me. "You look just about exhausted, Danny. Did they beat you with rubber hoses, or anything horrible?"

"My guess is they're saving that for the next time around!" I stood up real slow. "If you girls will excuse me, I'll—"

"Of course!" Shari said in a warm voice. "You go straight to bed, Danny, and get a good night's sleep!"

"Is there anything you want, like some hot soup, or milk?" Jackie inquired. "Aspirin, maybe?"

"Not a thing," I assured them, "and thanks again for everything. If I'm not around in the morning, call Lieutenant Schell, huh? He's sure to know exactly where I am!"

I went back to my room and made myself a drink. It was something they called a paradox, I thought numbly. On the one hand the wild alibi those two blondes had cooked up between them had saved me; but then they'd opened their big mouths too wide, and destroyed me on the other hand. For sure, Schell would have already dispatched a couple of the slugs taken out of Wayland's head to New York, for a ballistics comparison with the slug removed from Alysia Ames' head. The waking nightmare I'd had in Schell's office had become a reality, and how much time did that leave me? Until morning if I was lucky, I figured, and if not then no more than six hours. I gulped down the rest of my drink, collected the shoulder-harness from my suitcase and fitted it under my coat, then shoved the Thirty-eight I'd taken from Chuck MacKenzie into the armpit holster.

"Good evening, Mr. Boyd," a familiar voice said when I dropped my roomkey onto the front desk.

"Well, if it isn't my blackmailing friend, Sam Brickhouse?" I grinned at the desk clerk. "They banished you to the night shift?"

"A favor for a friend," he said with great dignity.

"You hear anything I could be interested in?" I asked, out of politeness.

"The police were looking for you at lunchtime," he whispered confidentially.

"They found me!" I grated. "So what else is new?"

He shrugged helplessly. "It's the night shift that dislocates my activities, Mr. Boyd!"

"Have you worked here long, Sam?" I asked.

"About five years. I've lived in Santo Bahia all my life, and I wouldn't trade it for anyplace else in the whole wide world."

"That's nice," I grunted. "You know a guy by the name of Chuck MacKenzie?"

"Sure," he nodded, "heads up the biggest construction—"

"Not that MacKenzie," I said patiently. "I'm talking about his son."

"I never knew he even had a son."

"He was in the Luau Room last night. Could be he's around the hotel a lot? A guy around thirty, average height and weight, with a kind of average face?" I saw the stunned look in his eyes and grinned reluctantly. "That's the whole problem, Sam, he's a very average-looking character!"

"We get a million guys who look like that walk through the lobby every day," he said helplessly.

"Every man has some kind of a unique quality about him," I said desperately. "You're a sensitive student of human nature, Sam; if I could only figure out what unique—" I snapped my fingers sharply "—it's his voice! Even when he's smiling and talking real polite, it's still there. A feeling of innate violence just below the surface the whole time. In a crazy kind of way it's like watching a tiger in a zoo; half the time it never even looks at the bars, but you know goddamn well if somebody removed a couple of bars the tiger would be outside the cage a split-second later."

The desk clerk took off his rimless glasses and polished the lens carefully with his pocket handkerchief, his face immobile like he was the last of the wooden Indians.

"Never mind, Sam," I said wearily.

He pushed his glasses back onto his nose, then his eyes suddenly shone like a pair of headlamps. "Got him!" he said excitedly. "You have a gift for a phrase, Mr. Boyd —a feeling of deep violence lurking beneath—" he chuckled happily "—and he's got these hooded eyes, right?"

"Right," I agreed.

"He was here just after I came on duty around two this afternoon, and he wanted the number of Mrs. Wayland's room."

"What did he say, exactly?"

"Asked me to call her and tell her an old family friend of her sister would like to visit with her for a few minutes, to talk about the family photographs. She sounded real surprised when I repeated what he'd said, then asked me to send him straight up to her room."

"Thanks, Sam." I dropped a sawbuck onto the desk.

"A pleasure doing business with you, anytime, Mr. Boyd."

I checked out the senior MacKenzie's home address, then had the doorman find me a cab. It stopped outside a substantial-looking Cape Cod in a quiet backstreet around ten minutes later and I told the driver to wait, then walked quickly up onto the front porch and rang the doorbell. Charlie MacKenzie opened the front door a few moments later, and a faint grin creased his battered face when he recognized me.

"Come on in, Danny," he rasped. "I was just about to make a drink."

The living room was pleasantly furnished but had that unlived-in feeling about it, which figured when a man lived alone. One item stood out from the rest because it did have a lived-in look about it, and that was the ornate bar built into one corner. MacKenzie pushed his bulk in back of the bartop and looked at me expectantly.

"A little rye, with a lot of ice," I told him. "I don't have much time, Charlie, so listen hard, huh?"

I told him Jackie's theory about how Wayland figured on borrowing the three million from himself, then, after the merger had gone through, finagling MacKenzie out of everything. His face was expressionless while he listened attentively, but his gray eyes grew steadily bleaker the whole time.

"Somebody killed the bastard early this morning, you know that?" I nodded, and he shrugged his massive shoulders. "If you'd told me this last night, I might have killed him myself. You have any idea who did it, Danny?"

"The same person who killed Alysia," I said.

"What kind of an answer is that?" He raised his eyebrows and gave me an amiable grin.

"I'm not too sure how you'll take this," I said in a neutral voice, "and I need your help real bad right now."

"Try me," he grunted.

"I figure a man called Charles MacKenzie the second, killed the both of them."

He lifted his glass to his mouth and drained it empty, without hurrying, then put the glass back down onto the bar and tilted the neck over the rim. "What kind of help?" he said.

"The pictures you took of Alysia with the four young athletes?" I said. "Whatever happened to them?"

"I destroyed them the day after the divorce came through."

"All of them?" I prodded.

He concentrated on tearing the cellophane wrapper off one of his outsized cigars for a moment. "There was one set missing. Maybe a couple of months before, somebody broke into the house during the daytime when I was out on the development. Nothing important seemed to be missing, so I didn't pay much attention to it at the time."

"It could have been Chuck?"

"I don't see why not?" He rubbed the back of his hand across his mouth quickly. "You remember I said I beat the hell out of him, destroyed all his personal possessions, then gave him five bucks and told him to get lost for the rest of his life?" He didn't bother waiting for my answer. "It wasn't strictly true. I didn't start in on his things until around a couple of weeks later. There was a book of poems he'd written—" an embarrassed look showed up on his face "—I never read anything like them in my whole life before. They were all dedicated to Alysia. The kid was wild crazy in love with her! The sex orgy hadn't been just a one-time thing like I'd figured before. It had been going on almost since the time I first married her." He shook his head slowly. "I tell you, Danny, it gave me a weird feeling to read those poems. It was like being able to see straight into a man's soul—the great soaring heights were there, and the bottomless pits right along-side!"

"And you figure if he loved her that much, he couldn't have killed her?" I prompted.

"I guess I do," he said. "Loving her the way he did, it just doesn't seem possible."

"Suppose something made her stop loving him?" I shrugged quickly. "That would have made it easy."

"Maybe?" He didn't sound convinced. "But if I'd known the whole truth at the time it happened, the chances are I wouldn't have been so hard on him."

I put my glass down on the bartop and stared hard at

102

him. After a few seconds his eyes flinched a little, then he grinned uneasily.

"So how can I help you, Danny-boy?"

"You've seen him," I said slowly. "Sometime between when we talked this morning, and now, you've seen him."

"Who?" he growled.

"The suddenly prodigal son," I snapped. "That's why you've just fed me all this crud about his poems, and how somebody burgled this house and stole a set of those pictures." The obvious explanation flashed into my mind. "He had to come to you today sometime after he'd killed Wayland because he needed a set of those pictures real bad. Without them, he couldn't get to Shari Wayland, right?"

"I don't know what the hell you're raving about," he rasped. "What I do know is I suddenly don't like you for a drinking partner anymore." His left arm flailed across the bartop and swept everything onto the floor, and it was real noisy there until the last glass had smashed. "I'll give you exactly five seconds to get the hell out of my house, Boyd," he said softly.

"I'm going," I told him. "But tell Chuck something from me? His partner said the wrong thing this morning and I'm about to follow through on that right now, because his partner is the weak half of the team." I grinned at MacKenzie. "He'll come apart at the seams in no time at all."

"You've got maybe a couple of seconds left," he grated.

"What did he offer in return for the pictures, Charlie? That you could take his place now that Wayland was dead? And you bought it, didn't you, Charlie? I guess that's why you're trying so goddamned hard to convince yourself he couldn't have killed Alysia, too?"

He made a wild animal kind of sound deep inside his

103

throat, grabbed the nearest full bottle off the shelf, and started around the bar toward me. I yanked the Thirty-eight out of the harness and rammed the barrel brutally hard into his stomach. It stopped him, but for a nasty moment there I figured it wasn't about to make any difference.

"I'm leaving now, Charlie," I said easily. "And don't forget to pass on my message to Chuck!"

"You know something, Boyd?" He spat some of the frothy saliva that coated his lips onto the nearest rug. "If my son doesn't get to you, I'll kill you myself!"

It was a thought to take out with me into the night. I told the cabdriver to head for the nearest drugstore, and wait for me again. I called Stanger's home number and asked to speak with him. A tired-sounding female voice said he wasn't home. I asked where I could reach him, and she said he was in an emergency conference at his office and none of them were taking any phone calls. The cabdriver seemed relieved when I told him the next stop would be the last. It was just after eight-thirty when he dropped me outside the offices of the *Strategic Development Corporation.*

A watchman tried to stop me entering the building until I told him I had some vital information Mr. Stanger was waiting for, and it would cost him his job if he didn't let me inside. Right then he offered to lead the way to the boardroom, but I said verbal directions would be just fine. When I got there, I stopped for a moment in the open doorway and watched. There was just the three of them; Stanger sitting at the head of the long polished table, the skin drawn so tight across his face it looked like a naked skull surmounted the neck of his shirt. Norman and Thatcher flanked him on either side, and Norman was talking so vehemently that none of them heard me walk into the room.

". . . and that's the way Stirling planned it," his high-pitched voice said with a sudden newly-found confidence. "Put the money into a separate bank account so MacKenzie would never realize he was actually borrowing from Stirling himself."

"It's all very fascinating, Ed," Thatcher grunted, "and its also history now Wayland is dead!"

"You're wrong, George!" The prominent apple in Norman's throat leaped suddenly with the passion in his voice. "Nothing is changed! In fact, it's a hell of a lot easier this way with me, instead of Stirling, handling the merger."

"The money, Ed!" Thatcher said irritably. "Stirling put the money in a separate bank account, you said? Who the hell will ever get it out again, except his trustees after the death taxes have been paid?"

Norman giggled triumphantly. "You haven't been listening to me, George. It doesn't need to come out before that. Not so long as whoever inherits the estate gives a firm guarantee the money will be put into the merger once it's free!"

"You know who inherits, Ed?" Thatcher asked softly.

"Not me," Norman giggled again. "Who else but the two women in his life—his wife—and his mistress?"

"Alysia's dead," Thatcher said.

"So practically all of the estate will go to Shari." Norman brought the flat of his hand down onto the tabletop with a gentle thump. "And I tell you right now, she'll guarantee the money for the merger!" He lifted his head up sharply, and the triumphant smile on his face suddenly froze when he saw me standing at the far end of the table.

"Hi, there, Ed!" I gave him the special warm friendly smile. "You made a small mistake this morning, but what else can you expect from a small man like you?"

105

"What the hell are you doing here, Boyd?" Thatcher snarled. "This is a private meeting, and you can get the hell out right now, or I'll throw you out bodily!"

"Shut up," I told him, and concentrated on Norman. "You don't remember?"

"Okay, you asked for it!" Thatcher took one step toward me quickly, then the sound of Stanger's voice stopped him again.

"Do stop playing these childish heroics, George," the reedy baritone said plaintively. "You seem to think you can resolve every problem by giving someone a punch on the nose! I'm very interested to hear what Mr. Boyd has to say."

"You know something, old man?" Thatcher almost choked on his own fury. "This merger could be real inside the next four weeks, and then you'll be looking for a job as a cleaner!"

"Until that time arrives, I'm still the president of this corporation," Stanger said acidly. "So sit down, George." Thatcher slid back into his chair and Stanger took time out to crack a couple of knuckles by way of a minor victory celebration. "Please continue, Mr. Boyd."

"I took the tape and the recorder back to my apartment that night in New York," I said. "Alysia Ames visited with me maybe an hour later with some kind of wild story that she was convinced the voice wasn't Wayland's at all, but someone had cleverly impersonated him. She managed to lift my gun from the bedroom and took it and the tape with her. But she left her evening purse behind, and it contained the keys to her apartment. I figured it was worth a try, anyway, so I went to her apartment later the same night. She was dead when I got there, and her murderer had used my gun to kill her, then left it on the floor. Both the tape and the recorder had gone."

"Deductions, Mr. Boyd?" Stanger asked in a soft voice.

106

"Who would know I'd lost possession of the tape?" I said. "Me, of course—Alysia's murderer, obviously—and maybe his partner?"

"Do we have to listen to this hysterical nonsense?" Norman said shrilly. "The man is either insane, or trying some kind of blackmail stunt!"

"After Alysia was found murdered, nobody whose name was mentioned on that tape would be exactly happy at the thought it could be turned over to the police at anytime," I said. "Even if they were entirely innocent, it would be worth paying out some money to ensure the tape was destroyed. You figured it was worth five hundred dollars, as I remember?"

"I was limited by the amount of ready cash available," Stanger said dryly.

"George doubled your bid to a thousand dollars," I said.

"Sure I did, but what the hell?" Thatcher asked angrily. "The way you tell it, all *that* proved was my innocence, right?"

"Absolutely right," I agreed. "Either of you gentlemen remember precisely how much Ed Norman bid for the tape?"

During the short silence that followed, Norman sat rigid in his chair while blind fear locked his facial muscles into a kind of obscene parody of a death mask.

"Ed?" Thatcher said in a wondering voice. "He said he wasn't interested, and he didn't even bid a goddamned solitary dime!"

"The look on Norman's face is proof beyond a doubt of what you've told us, Mr. Boyd," Stanger said. "But are you suggesting he was the one who murdered the Ames girl?"

"Ed was only the junior partner," I said, and couldn't keep the contempt out of my voice, "like always!"

Norman put his arms onto the tabletop, then cradled his head in them in a curiously childlike gesture as if, by blotting out sight and sound, he could also blot out the whole cruel world around him.

"So, who did kill Alysia?" Thatcher asked abruptly.

"You mean who killed both Alysia and Stirling Wayland?" I corrected him. "The answer is Charles Mac-Kenzie the second—commonly known as, Chuck—MacKenzie's son."

"I never even knew he had a son." Stanger sounded mildly surprised.

"You've both met him," I said. "In Wayland's Sutton Place penthouse, the night we all heard the tape played. Remember the butler who was so fast with a gun?"

"Him?" Thatcher's mouth dropped open. "But how? —I mean, I figured he was working with you?"

"Everybody, especially me, was meant to think that," I said, then pulled out a chair and sat down facing Stanger across the length of the table. "It's been one hell of a day! You think I could have a drink?"

"Sure." Thatcher got up quickly. "I'll fix it, I could use one myself. How about you, Kurt?"

"Not now," Stanger shook his head.

"Back in a moment," Thatcher said. "Is bourbon okay?"

"Fine," I told him. "On the rocks?"

The moment he left the room I took the Thirty-eight out of the harness, put it flat on the tabletop and gave it a push. It slid easily across the highly-polished surface, and Norman's buried head didn't even twitch as it passed him. Stanger cupped his hand and the gun slid gently into it, then he looked at me with an inquiring expression on his face.

"I do hope this is not some subtle hint that I should blow my brains out, or something?"

I grinned. "It's some kind of insurance, I hope! Would

108

you mind just slipping the gun into your pocket, Mr. Stanger?"

"Anything you say, Mr. Boyd." He dropped the gun into his coat pocket. "I must say this all seems highly dramatic. Are you seriously expecting some kind of violence to take place here in the boardroom?"

"Any moment now," I said truthfully.

"The last time, as I remember, I witnessed any violence was in Okinawa in 1945." He shook his head slowly. "It all seems a long time back."

Thatcher came into the room carrying the drinks on a tray and, by the way it jumped in his hands, it looked like he had a sudden palsy. In back of him, the barrel of his gun pressed tight against the nape of Thatcher's neck, was Chuck MacKenzie.

"I came as soon as I got your message, Boyd." He chuckled softly. "Whatever did you say to my old man? I've never seen him so mad since that day he caught me and my buddies taking Alysia—" he chuckled again "—in turn!"

Chapter
TEN

He stopped about five feet away from me, then the gunbarrel swung in my direction. Thatcher put the tray down onto the table, then slumped into the nearest chair and began to mop the sweat from his face.

"I'll have your gun, Boyd, butt-first," Chuck said crisply.

"No gun," I told him.

"You pulled one on the old man less than an hour

back." His cold hooded eyes raked my face. "So what happened, you ate it?"

"I ditched it outside," I said. "I'm in enough trouble with the local fuzz already! If I kill anybody now—even with ten eye-witnesses to swear it was self-defense—Lieutenant Schell won't be about to believe it." I pulled my coat open wide so he could see the empty shoulder harness. "I tossed the gun into the bushes out in front of the main entrance."

"Maybe." He nodded toward Thatcher. "I know he's clean because I frisked him outside." Then he looked hard at Stanger who was sitting placidly at the head of the table, his hands in front of him. "You gave it to the old man, Boyd?" Chuck said softly.

"Oh, sure!" I said. "Mr. Stanger figures the arthritis hasn't hardly affected his aim at all. He does have a little problem trying to bend his fingers around the gunbutt, but then nobody's perfect!"

Stanger cracked his knuckles in rapid succession, and the noise sounded like a minor fusillade of gunshots. "Mr. Boyd said I was to shoot you through the back of the head the moment your attention was distracted," he told Chuck. "I do hope you'll come a little closer to this end of the table first."

"Okay, Boyd," Chuck said in an almost amiable voice. "It makes sense you're scared of the local fuzz, because I killed Stirling with your own gun." He grinned savagely. "It was real nice of you to switch guns on me! You must have figured I was completely stupid and wouldn't notice, huh? There was only one thing to do with a murder weapon that didn't belong to me, and that was use it for a second murder, then leave it beside the body so the fuzz could check out its real owner!" The grin vanished suddenly. "So what did you hope to achieve by bringing me here when you were unarmed?"

110

"The only way a conspiracy can work is by keeping it that way," I told him. "I just blew your conspiracy right here, Chuck. They—" I nodded toward Thatcher and Stanger "—know all about it now."

He looked at Norman, who still had his head completely buried in his arms. "Breaking down Ed must have been tough!" he said. "Like cracking a soft-boiled egg, even? Go and sit beside the old man at the other end of the table, Boyd. That way I don't have to go crosseyed the whole time.'

I did as I was told, collecting my drink on the way. The moment after I took the chair Thatcher had vacated when he went to get the drinks, Chuck helped himself to a drink then took the chair I had vacated at the end of the table.

"I underestimated you, Boyd," he said thoughtfully. "So now I want you to spell it out, the way you see it, from the very beginning." There was a dreamy quality to his voice for a moment. "I guess I don't have to tell you how much depends on you doing this right?"

"In the beginning Stirling Wayland was married to a girl whose name had been Ames before they were married," I said. "Then your father married her sister, Alysia. After a while it got that Wayland hated his wife because he wanted her as his slave, and she wouldn't go along with that. During the time she still trusted him, she asked would he keep an eye on her kid sister and he did —through you?"

"I'd gotten involved in a little trouble and needed some cash fast," he said. "The old man would have flipped if I'd gone to him, and I knew Wayland was Alysia's brother-in-law so I went to him instead. The money was no problem to Stirling, and he made sure we became real buddies. After a while he realized just how much I hated my old man's guts, so he came up with a proposition. He

111

wanted Alysia as a mistress so he could flaunt her in front of his wife, without Shari being able to do a god-damned thing about it. If I could organize it so the old man divorced her, it was worth twenty thousand dollars to him. If I could organize it so the circumstances really stank, there was a five grand bonus in for me." He shrugged easily. "It wasn't hard; Alysia was thirty years younger than the old man, anyway. The first time I made a pass at her, she practically seduced me."

"And your three buddies?" I queried.

"Maybe you know she wasn't quite right in her head?" His casual tone of voice belied the raw brutality of the question. "And when she'd been drinking it made her even wilder than ever. So I set it up with her that week-end, and got one of my buddies to make an anonymous phone-call to the old man. Like you know, he threw the both of us out of the house after taking some messy pic-tures of the proceedings first. I took her straight into Wayland's waiting arms, collected my twenty-five grand and went into the construction business in a small way."

"Around San Diego?" I prodded.

"I had a little trouble there," he allowed, "and most of my stake money had gotten used up. Then I heard about the big island development starting back here, with the old man doing most of the construction. One thing I had learned down San Diego way was how to louse up a proj-ect real good. I got to thinking about that, and the idea of sending the old man bankrupt began to appeal to me. Then I figured why stop there? So I went to Wayland, told him my idea, and he was for it." He frowned sud-denly. "Hold it! I told *you* to spell it out, Boyd!"

"You outlined a plan to sabotage the entire project, send both *Strategic* and your old man broke before the project was completed, then have Wayland take the lot over," I said. "Wayland knew his junior partner, Ed Norman, and Thatcher, the executive vice-president of *Strategic* were old buddies, so for a cut of the ultimate profit and the presidency of the new company after a merger, Thatcher would join the conspiracy."

"Not bad," Chuck nodded. "What then?"

"You always were ambitious," I said slowly. "After a while you started to think about Wayland. Why should he, instead of you, get the thick slice off the top? So you made a friend out of Ed Norman, told him how unfair it was that a brilliant guy like him should be kept in a junior and subservient position by Wayland. So Norman became your partner—he thought—and in the meantime you kept up your special relationship with Alysia whenever Wayland wasn't around and you were."

"I find myself getting a little confused right here, Mr. Boyd," Stanger ventured in his reedy baritone.

"We haven't even started yet!" I told him, then concentrated on Chuck again. "How did you find out the detail of Wayland's will—through Alysia?"

"Sure. I told her to put on a screaming fit with Stirling one time, and ask what would happen to her if he unfortunately dropped dead the next day? She kept it up for so long he finally showed her the will."

"My guess is you made an apparent attempt on Wayland's life, to scare the hell out of him at the right moment?" I said.

"I'm very good with a handgun." He grinned briefly. "One night when I was supposed to be playing poker with some old buddies—who'd give me an alibi if needed—I waited until he got out of his car at the motel we were staying in—then put a bullet past his ear. When I supposedly arrived home from the poker game an hour later he was still gibbering with terror!"

"Then you convinced him it could only be one of five people who had tried to kill him, and the best deterrent would be some record of that—like the tape recording?"

"I could take it back to New York at the weekend when we knew all five of them would be there, make like a butler at the party he had supposedly invited them to, and play the tape. The only thing was, I told him we needed to be goddamned sure the tape was kept in a safe place afterward, so why not hire a good private detective?"

"How come you got me?"

"I advised Wayland to ask the local fuzz if they knew of a good private detective in New York. Your buddy, Schell, recommended you."

"Wasn't that taking a risk, involving a professional outsider in your schemes?" Stanger asked.

"The way Chuck had it figured out I was an absolute necessity," I said grimly. "He needed a ready-made murderer!"

"You know what happened the night of the party," Chuck said amiably. "After you'd left, Boyd, I called Alysia and told her to get that tape back from you anyway she could, but deliberately leave her purse with her house keys in it behind. I was waiting for her at the apartment when she got back, and when she handed me your gun it was like Santa Claus visiting in July."

"Why did you need to kill her, Chuck?" I asked politely.

"She was expendable," he said simply, "and what a drag she would have been after Wayland was dead!" He leaned forward across the end of the table with an incredible look of dedication on his face. "The most important thing in this kind of deal is to think ahead, Boyd. Wayland's estate split down the middle between his wife and mistress. An unnecessary complication! So eliminate one of them before you eliminate him, was the obvious answer. It didn't matter which one, it was only a matter of choice. Alysia was an obvious choice; for one thing

114

you never know what a dame who hasn't got all her marbles will do under pressure, and I also knew I could use her background to get Shari thinking my way afterward."

"So you killed her with my gun, took the tape with you and—" I stopped short for a moment "—why didn't you call the cops right then and have me caught redhanded at the scene of the crime?"

"Because you hadn't committed the second murder yet," he said patiently, like he was talking to a small child. "I wanted you right here in Santo Bahia, knowing somebody had tried to frame you for Alysia's murder, and worrying like crazy, Boyd! It had been real easy to persuade Wayland to hole up in that shack, while I checked out the situation for him, so I knew there was no chance of him running interference. Last night I told you that crud about you being fired to panic you a little more." He rubbed his forehead gently with his free hand. "And I haven't forgotten that little episode out on the development, either! Afterward, when I found you'd switched guns on me, it was like Santa Claus just couldn't stop visiting with me!"

"So you killed Wayland sometime early this morning with my gun, and left it beside the body again but this time—unlike the time in New York—you gave the fuzz an anonymous tip-off?" I said.

There was a faintly puzzled look on his face. "What I don't understand is why you aren't behind bars right now?"

"I had an alibi," I said, "and that's the reason your whole plan is blown sky-high, Chuck!"

"No," he shook his head confidently. "It just needed some revision, is all. I had to go to the old man for a set of those pictures, so I could convince Shari to guarantee the money for the merger after probate's granted on Wayland's will. You'd be amazed how much a man's moral fibers will bend under the pressure of imminent bankruptcy! In

115

return for a piece of the new company, after the merger has gone through, the old man is a hundred per cent on my side." His hooded eyes searched my face quickly, then he gave a contented grin. "I can see you got the same impression when you visited with him a little time back, huh?"

"Even so, it won't work," I snarled. "Like I said before, Chuck, a conspiracy is only good so long as it stays a conspiracy. It's finished the moment the wrong people get to know about it. People like me, and Mr. Stanger here."

"When I said I'd revised my plans, I did mean a complete revision and not just some off-the-cuff adjustment," he said in a hurt voice. "I do wish you'd stop underestimating me, Boyd, the same way I stopped underestimating you! Let me briefly explain how the fuzz will see the whole situation. Wayland was convinced his mistress was trying to kill him, so he hired you to kill her first. Then Wayland refused to pay-off and in desperation—anger? —you killed him. They had to let you go because you produced an alibi, but you knew as soon as they matched the slug that killed Alysia in New York with the slugs that killed Wayland in Santo Bahia, you were a dead pigeon! So in desperation you came to Stanger, here tonight, and told him that by killing Wayland you'd saved him from being the victim of a gigantic fraud. In return, you wanted a few thousand dollars you could use for a getaway. Stanger very properly refused to give it to you, so then you killed him in a fit of rage and frustration."

"You can't be for real, Chuck!" I grinned broadly at him. "It's so full of holes you couldn't float it in an oil bath!"

"Take all the time you want, friend," he said evenly. "I'd be glad to hear the weaknesses?"

"I presume it means you're going to kill Stanger right here in this room, in front of witnesses?"

116

"And kill you right afterward," he added coldly.

"Then kill the two witnesses after that?" I grinned derisively at him. "Four corpses will take a hell of a lot of explaining!"

"I need those witnesses real bad," he said. "Almost as bad as they need me! You know something, Boyd? Without me to influence Shari Wayland, the poor widow-lady, into guaranteeing the money for the merger, there won't be any merger or any new company. Without the new company, both George and Ed will be out of a job, instead of being the new president, and vice-president respectively. As well as stockholders, too!"

"They'll have to be about the most reliable witnesses you can get," I snarled. "They'll be holding your life in their clammy little hands, Chuck!"

"I'm sure I can rely on George here," he said, and that weird dream-like quality crept into his voice again. "I know I can rely on the other witness implicitly, because he'll be myself."

"How about Norman?" I grunted.

"Didn't I tell you?" He waited a couple of seconds, savoring his punch line. "Ed is the hero of this little melodrama. The brave man who, unfortunately, is a split-second too late when he tries to save Stanger's life by shooting you."

"Look at him." I pointed at Norman whose head was still cradled tight in his arms. "*He* looks like a hero?"

"You don't know much about heroes, do you?" His voice hardened again. "Ed looks exactly like a hero—the Mr. Average Man unused to violence—who performs a sudden act of heroism when he tries to prevent a murder, then falls apart emotionally when he realizes he's killed a man!"

There was just the one chance left. "How about it, George?" I asked. "Are you going along with this?"

Thatcher ran one hand slowly through his wiry black

hair, then came the blinding flash as he bared his white teeth in a nervous grin.

"Show me one good reason why I shouldn't go along with Chuck," he said.

"You're making yourself an accessory before the act to murder," I grated. "Equal guilt and equal responsibility, George."

"It's the chance I take if I want to be the president, and a stockholder, of the new company after the merger," he said slowly. "The alternative is remain where I am, the executive vice-president of a company about to be bankrupt. That's a hell of a good reference for another executive position!" He shook his head tightly. "I'm sorry about you and Kurt, Boyd, but it's not about to keep me awake nights."

"Any last requests, Boyd?" Chuck asked politely. "You want to plead with me? Cry a little, maybe? Smoke a cigarette?"

Stanger cracked one knuckle loudly. "I would like to make sure I have you in the correct perspective, Mr. MacKenzie." he said in a formal voice. "You murdered Alysia Ames, and also murdered Stirling Wayland this morning?"

"Speak up, old man!" Chuck snapped. "Because real soon nobody will be able to hear you!"

"And now you propose to murder myself and Mr. Boyd? Purely for the sake of money?"

"And power," Chuck murmured. "Money I can always get, one way or the other. But power? That's something different!"

"I guess you have your answer, Mr. Stanger," I said.

"I know I have," he said softly, "and now, I suppose the time has come to meet our fate, Mr. Boyd?"

"Maybe we should check and find out if the vote is

118

unanimous first?" I leaned across the table and shouted, "Hey, *Norman!*"

He lifted his head slowly and there was a dull withdrawn look in his eyes as he stared at me vacantly. I came out of my chair fast, grabbed a fistful of his lapels with my left hand and pulled him across the tabletop toward me. Then I hit him across the point of his jaw with all the weight I could put in back of my right fist. His eyes glazed, then he fell backward onto his chair, which tilted past the point of no return with the momentum, and sent him crashing to the floor.

"You stupid bastard, Boyd!" Chuck's voice quivered with fury. "That doesn't alter a thing!"

"Maybe it does?" I stepped back from the table grabbed the chair in both hands, and swung it over my head. "You'll have to call the cops real fast the moment after you shoot either one of us, because the night watchman inside the building will come running the moment he hears the shot." I started toward him slowly, the chair still held over my head. "So right now you just can't afford to pull that trigger, right?"

"You moron!" He spat the word at me. "All I have to do is switch heroes, so George becomes the brave man, while Norman was so overcome with fear he passed out cold! But you never even thought of that, Boyd!" The tight grin on his face became a fixed grimace, as the barrel of his gun traversed maybe an inch so it was pointing directly at my chest again. "And I hope this hurts like hell!"

The sound of the two shots reverberated around the room, while Chuck stood there with a look of absolute disbelief frozen on his face. Then the gun spilled out of his hand, bounced once on the tabletop, then fell to the floor. His left hand pawed his chest and was instantly stained a reddish-brown color the moment before he plunged face-forward onto the tabletop, then lay still.

Stanger put the gun down in front of him carefully, then cracked four fingers without hurrying. "I was hoping for a diversion, and you didn't disappoint me, Mr. Boyd," he said in his reedy baritone. "It was very nicely done, very nicely indeed!"

"Okinawa?" I queried.

"An acting colonel in an infantry division." His mouth stretched a little at the corners. "I must show you my sharpshooter's medal sometime."

Thatcher made one last attempt to mop his face with an already saturated handkerchief. "I wouldn't have gone along with him, not for a moment," he said shakily. "You both understand that, of course! I had an idea you two were up to something, so the best thing I could do would be just pretend to agree, right?"

"There is one thing, Mr. Stanger," I said, carefully ignoring the frantic pleading look on Thatcher's face. "I've gotten to know Shari Wayland real well over the last couple of days. Now, of course, there's no point in any merger, so there won't be any new company. But I'm sure she'll agree to loaning *Strategic* the necessary money to see the development project through, and give you a written guarantee on that until the will's probated."

I walked down to where Chuck's body lay across the table and went through his pockets as delicately as I could, until I found the set of pictures. One look at the first one was enough. I put them into my inside pocket, then looked at Stanger again.

"Charlie MacKenzie may have more of these," I said. "I'm sure he'll see the point about giving them to you for instant destruction, in return for the chance of *Strategic* paying the money it owes him?" I shrugged my shoulders gently. "I just had the idea this could influence your thinking about the future of your executive vice-president."

"It does indeed, Mr. Boyd." His cadaverous-looking

120

face had a purely bland look as he concentrated on Thatcher. "Run, don't walk, out of this building, George," he said softly. "Mail me your resignation first thing in the morning, and don't look for any severance pay! Don't even look for a job as a cleaner, George, because there'll never be a vacancy for you!"

Thatcher opened his mouth wide, saw the look in Stanger's eyes, and closed it abruptly again. Then he got to his feet and walked out of the office in a kind of somnambulistic glide.

"No watchman?" I said.

Stanger checked his strap watch. "He should be way over the other side of the building at this time, and the sound of the shots wouldn't carry that far."

"I'm glad Chuck didn't know that," I grinned.

"I suppose I should resent your having made me kill a man tonight," he said thoughtfully. "But somehow I don't; it seemed more like a public service when I pulled the trigger! Now—" his voice became brisk "—are you going to call this Lieutenant Schell, or shall I?"

"You call him," I whimpered. "*Please!*"

Chapter
ELEVEN

I stared at the wall above his head and got no inspiration from its color of old dried blood at all. "What time is it?" I asked.

"Ten after two," Schell snapped. "Why?"

"A.M.?"

"What the hell else?"

"The way I feel we could have been here a couple of days already, what with you asking the same goddamned stupid questions over and over again," I snarled.

His fingers beat a soft tattoo on the battered desktop. "One of these days, Boyd!" He closed his eyes for a couple of seconds. "One thing still bugs me; where did the gun Stanger used to kill MacKenzie come from in the first place?"

"Didn't he tell you?" I asked carefully.

"He was vague." Schell glowered at me. "I asked him the same question five times and got five different answers, and they were all vague!"

"Talking of guns," I said conversationally, "can I have my own gun back now?"

He swallowed hard. "When we're all through with it!"

"If I'd had it with me tonight," I said sorrowfully, "I could have loaned it to Stanger."

"Thank your miserable hide you didn't have any gun with you tonight," he grated. "If it had been you who killed MacKenzie, I wouldn't have believed one goddamned word of the whole story, and never mind who else was there to corroborate it!"

"Can I go now?" I asked wearily.

"I guess so. I'm sick of seeing your stupid face around here, anyway. And get the hell back to New York where you belong, and real soon! You hear me, Boyd!"

"The way you're shouting, I'd figure about half the town's population can hear you." I got to my feet, then edged toward the door. "It never is nice meeting you again, Lieutenant, so saying goodbye is the best part. I was going to bring suit for false arrest, but then I figured you've got enough troubles already."

"Just tell me one thing before you go?"

122

For a moment there, I couldn't believe it but there was a definite look of embarrassment on his face. "Well," I shrugged. "There's no harm in you asking, anyway."

"That alibi those two dames gave you?" He seemed to be having some difficulty mouthing the words. "It wasn't true, was it?"

I looked at him coldly. "Lieutenant, I'm surprised at you! How could you ever doubt the word of two real honest girls like them?"

"You mean—" for some occult reason he was now breathing heavily "—the both of them—and you—were in the same—and for the whole night?"

"I guess it's mainly a question of physical fitness," I said modestly, "and a certain attitude of mind."

He banged his elbows onto the desktop, then supported his head in his hands. "Just go," he said in a muffled voice. "Now! Like before my mind becomes completely unhinged."

By the time I got back to my hotel room it was getting close to three A.M. and I figured I'd never felt so bushed in my whole life before. A long tepid shower relaxed me a little, then I put on a robe and decided a nightcap could help ease my weary bones. It didn't seem worth the effort to wait for some ice cubes to come up from room service, so I poured what was left in the rye bottle into a glass and topped it up with water. I was about halfway through the drink when there was a soft tap on the door. For a moment there I twitched badly, then I remembered Chuck MacKenzie was refrigerating in the morgue, so what the hell did I have to twitch about?

I opened the door a moment later and two blondes walked into the room. There was an uneasy prickling at the nape of my neck the moment after I closed the door and looked at them. Maybe it had something to do with the way they were looking at me with the identical smug, almost predatory smile on their faces? The bourbon-colored blonde was wearing the black silk robe, belted tightly around the waist, she had worn the previous night. The strawberry-blonde was wearing a blue silk robe, also belted tightly around the waist.

"We gave you around six hours, Danny," Shari purred.

"And we were right," Jackie cooed. "Look! You're all rested, and everything!"

"Isn't that great?" Shari said enthusiastically.

"Just great!" Jackie echoed.

"It's real nice of you two girls to visit," I said. "But it so happens I'm just out of liquor and I was figuring on—"

"Never mind about the liquor," Jackie said in a disdainful voice. "Who needs it?"

"We don't," Shari purred. "That's for sure."

"If you don't want a drink?" I smiled nervously at them, while I let the question hang in the air.

"We got to thinking," Shari said in a serious voice. "After what happened last night, who knows what might happen tonight?"

"It's just not worth taking the chance," Jackie agreed in a determined voice. "It was up to us, we decided. If Danny Boyd needed protection from that dreadful Schell man, then we weren't going to fail him in his hour of need!"

"No personal sacrifice would be too great!" Shari said emotionally. "Am I right, Jackie?"

"You are just about the most rightest person I ever heard being right!" Jackie said fondly. "Shall we?"

"Let's!" Shari exhaled slowly.

Then she unbelted her robe, pulled it off and tossed it carelessly over the arm of the nearest chair. Underneath

124

was just Shari in all her naked magnificence. While my mouth still hung open wide, Jackie unbelted her blue robe, pulled it off, and tossed it carelessly over the other arm of the chair. Underneath was just Jackie in all her naked magnificence. Then the two of them sauntered over to the bed, and the sight of their delicately jiggling bottoms made me feel almost frantic with frustration. If only I didn't feel so completely bushed! They plumped the cushions first, then lay down side by side on the bed, their hands cradled behind their heads, and smiled warmly at me.

"It's—uh!" My mouth suddenly dried so I frantically swallowed the rest of my drink. "I mean—"

"It was that horrible man and the way he obviously felt we were lying," Jackie said, in some kind of an occult explanation.

"Suppose you need an alibi for tonight, Danny?" Shari said softly. "That horrible lieutenant! I wouldn't put it past him to sneak right into your room and check!"

"And when he does," Jackie chuckled triumphantly, "he'll find the three of us altogether, right?"

"So be a good boy and come to bed, Danny," Shari said throatily. "The light is hurting my eyes."

"I'll switch it off," Jackie said, and did so. A second later she chuckled in the darkness. "I guess he was too modest to take his robe off before?"

"Watch out for the whirlwind!" Shari chuckled companionably. "He'll probably take a standing jump at us!"

My questing hand found the doorknob, turned it gently, then pulled the door open wide. I went across the hallway faster than a homing missile, heading toward Jackie's room. The moment I got inside I slammed the door shut and turned the key in the lock. I leaned my back against the door and waited for my breathing to return to something like normal, then heard a real strange sound. It took a while to realize it was in my mind—and it could only be an impression at that!—because I'd never heard Lieutenant Schell screaming with laughter in my whole life before!

Other SIGNET Suspense Fiction You Will Enjoy

☐ **ODDS ON by John Lange.** A unique mystery, in which three ingenious gentlemen utilize an IBM computer to mastermind a million dollar heist. (#P3068—60¢)

☐ **THE HOUSE OF BRASS by Ellery Queen.** Hendrik Brass invites six total strangers to his ancestral home in order to make them his heirs. When a murder occurs, it becomes difficult to find the murderer since each of them reveals a very plausible reason for committing the crime. (#T3831—75¢)

☐ **GIDEON'S RISK by J. J. Marric.** The incomparable Commander Gideon risks his career to trap the most elusive of criminals, the respectable and influential citizen. "A whirl of tenterhooks, arranged with practical skill." —**New York Herald Tribune** (#P3143—60¢)

☐ **MURDER AMONG CHILDREN by Tucker Coe.** Mitchell Tobin deals with a violent death and terror among a group of people in Greenwich Village. (#P4030—60¢)

☐ **THE CHAIRMAN by Jay Richard Kennedy.** A teacher turned agent is sent on a dangerous assignment to China to find a "destruction machine." A major motion picture starring Gregory Peck. (#P4007—60¢)

THE NEW AMERICAN LIBRARY, INC., P.O. Box 2310, Grand Central Station, New York, New York 10017

Please send me the SIGNET BOOKS I have checked above. I am enclosing $_____(check or money order—no currency or C.O.D.'s). Please include the list price plus 10¢ a copy to cover mailing costs. (New York City residents add 6% Sales Tax. Other New York State residents add 3% plus any local sales or use taxes).

Name_____

Address_____

City_____State_____ Zip Code_____
Allow at least 3 weeks for delivery